RIVERBOAT RENEGADE

Riverboat gambler Darcy Kane was a devil with the women, quick with gun or knife and faster still with a card. However, there were those who tried to fleece him. Then, when one man labelled him a cheat, and died for it, Darcy became known as the Killer. He exchanged the riverboat for a horse, carrying with him his deck of cards — his passport to the gambling men who were his quarry. His hopes lay with one woman, for surely she would help. Or was she the most corrupt of them all?

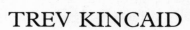

TREV KINCAID

RIVERBOAT RENEGADE

Complete and Unabridged

LINFORD
Leicester

First hardcover edition published in Great Britain
in 2003 by Robert Hale Limited, London

Originally published in paperback as
Riverboat Renegade by Chuck Adams

First Linford Edition
published 2004
by arrangement with
Robert Hale Limited, London

British Library CIP Data

Kincaid, Trev
  Riverboat renegade.—Large print ed.—
  Linford western library
  1. Western stories 2. Large type books
  I. Title II. Adams, Chuck
  823.9'14 [F]
  ISBN 1–84395–458–3

Published by
F. A. Thorpe (Publishing)
Anstey, Leicestershire

Set by Words & Graphics Ltd.
Anstey, Leicestershire
Printed and bound in Great Britain by
T. J. International Ltd., Padstow, Cornwall

This book is printed on acid-free paper

1

The Killing

'I'll see you, pardner,' said the man in the ten-gallon hat.

He seemed pleased with himself. The little eyes in the heavy red face glittered with triumph. This is where I get my money back and a whole lot more besides, the eyes seemed to say.

Darcy Kane took his time. He was busy lighting a long, thin, evil-smelling cheroot.

The cheroot was all part of his get-up, his uniform. The black broadcloth suit with wide lapels trimmed in braid. The soft black leather shoes. The white silk cravat with pearl stickpin. The gold and red flowered waistcoat. The gold watchchain that bisected the broad chest. The lean poker-face with the hooded eyes. The black hair worn rather long, curling round the ears and at the nape of the neck.

These were the time-honoured trappings of the professional gambler. The riverboat gambler no less: usually a more gentlemanly character than his brother from further West, who had to depend on horseflesh to take him from place to place instead of the stately elegance of a boat on the broad Mississippi.

Darcy got his cheroot going. He squinted through the blue smoke at the other occupants of the table. There were six of them. Four of them were bosom friends of the man in the ten-gallon hat. They all professed to be cattle-dealers. They had plenty of money with them.

Darcy, whose profession had made him a good judge of human nature, didn't completely believe the cattle-dealer story. Whatever they were, this bunch had certainly made a killing some place.

They were not good card-players and

they were ugly losers. They had already lost a pile to Darcy. The man in the ten-gallon hat had lost most of all. He had a good hand now judging by his manner. But Darcy had an idea that he again had a damn sight better one.

Darcy; the man in the ten-gallon hat; his four pardners. Six players. And the seventh, another professional like Darcy. Fancy Jack.

A little man with a pale face and a pot-belly. Dressed up like a strutting peacock: bottle-green velvet coat, gaudily flowered cravat, red silk cummerbund. A man who lived by his wits, the quickness of his tongue: a sleek, wriggling worm. Also — and Darcy was pretty sure about this now — a cheat. A cardsharp, which Darcy, having his own code, definitely was not. Although he was the slickest gambler on the river, he always played it straight. He had a reputation for his square-dealing, but these five ginks, being strangers, wouldn't know that. Fancy Jack knew it all right. But it wouldn't cut any ice with him.

Fancy Jack was winning, but not nearly so much as Darcy. If there was any trouble Darcy couldn't expect any help from that worm.

Darcy could see the way things were drifting. This was an ugly bunch he had gotten himself mixed up with. Being by nature an easy-going cuss who hated trouble unless it could be avoided, he was beginning to wish he hadn't joined this table at all.

'What're you waiting for?' said the man in the ten-gallon hat.

His voice was ugly. His demeanour had changed. His little eyes were wary now. He scowled all over his ugly face.

Darcy didn't like being pushed. He turned his cards over.

'Beat that then, friend,' he said silkily.

Blood flushed into the other man's heavy face. His eyes popped.

With a sweep of his hand he sent his own cards skittling across the table, scattering the chips and ashtrays. 'You cheated me,' he said thickly, as if the words were choking him, as if he had wanted to say them for a long time.

He shot to his feet as if he had been jerked upwards by the sudden pull of a rawhide rope. His chair went over with a clatter. He went for the gun, low-slung at his hip.

★   ★   ★

Darcy carried his small pistol in a shoulder-holster under his armpit. He saw the killing madness in the other man's eyes.

Darcy drew from a seated position.

The other man's Colt had barely cleared leather when Darcy's slug hit him in the forehead. He went over backwards, crashed on top of his own fallen chair. He was dead before he had stopped falling.

Darcy was on his feet now.

He covered the rest of the occupants of the table.

'You all saw that,' he said. 'He went for his gun first. I shot him in self-defence. Put your hands on the top of the table, all of you. You too, Jack.'

'I don't want any trouble with you, Darcy, you know that,' said Fancy Jack.

One of the men, lean with squint-eyes in a yellow face, spoke up now.

'You not only cheated him, you shot him down in cold blood.'

'He cheated us all,' said another of the cattle buyers.

'You're lying in your teeth, both of you,' said Darcy. 'I play a straight game. Everybody on the river knows that.'

Fancy Jack said nothing. Neither did the other two men.

They sat around the table, poised, their hands supine on the top. As if they were waiting for another kind of game to start.

People stared from other tables. People were half on their feet. But there was silence now. As if the whole room was suspended in a moment of time.

Then everybody suddenly started to talk at once. Some people there knew Darcy and began to back him up. But the dead man's four friends, those closest to the scene of the incident, were vociferous in their condemnation of a 'cold-blooded killing'. The word 'Cheat' was bandied about pretty freely too.

They did not move. They kept their hands on top of the table. But they wagged their jaws a mile a moment.

Darcy Kane's lean handsome face remained as impassive as ever. Only the glitter of his dark eyes betrayed his feelings.

He said: 'Take their guns, Jack.'

'Look here, Darcy . . . '

'Take their guns, Jack,' said Darcy silkily.

'All right, Darcy.'

Fancy Jack did as he was told.

'Now put them carefully in the centre of the table . . . And your own as well.'

'I didn't say anything, Darcy. I . . . '

'Don't argue with me, Jack.'

'All right, Darcy.'

Somebody had sent for the captain

and he now arrived. He was a comparatively new man on the river and Darcy only knew him vaguely, knew his name was Brunello. He'd heard about him though. That he was the son of a once-powerful but now impoverished Creole family, that he was a martinet, that though he acknowledged gamblers as part of riverlife, he didn't like too many of them on his boat.

He was fortyish, tall, darkly olive-skinned. He was well-built and upright and sported jet-black handlebar moustaches. With his peaked cap and blue suit he looked every inch a skipper. He was a good one it was said, if rather standoffish, never hail-fellow-well-met with the passengers as most other skippers on the river were.

He got down on one knee beside the fallen man. This could only be a mere formal act, for the man was so obviously dead, his ten-gallon hat lying behind his head, stained with blood and a rapidly widening red pool marring the Turkish carpet.

Captain Brunello rose, dusting off one knee of his impeccably pressed navy-blue trousers. Not for him the conglomeration of garments worn by some other skippers. He was a proud man with a cold sort of arrogance.

He turned towards the table and the dead man's friends began their complaints and accusations again.

The captain had brought three hefty-looking roustabouts with him. At a sign they moved forward, ranged themselves around the table. Darcy Kane had lowered his pistol and stood there, waiting.

The four men quit their jabber, watched the newcomers warily.

Captain Brunello faced Darcy, held out his hand palm upwards.

'Give me the gun, Kane,' he said.

This was the river, a river boat, a floating town with its own law. And, rightly so, the captain was that law. Slowly Darcy handed over his pistol.

'It was self-defence, cap'n,' he said.

'You will see that his hand's still on his gun and that it's almost out of its holster.'

The dead man's four friends started up with their arguments once more.

'*Quiet!*'

Brunello's voice cracked like a whiplash.

Then, still looking at Darcy, the captain said flatly, 'I shall have to lock you in your cabin until this thing has been investigated.'

Now he pointed Darcy's own gun negligently at him. 'Macell — Bull — take him away.'

Two of the sailors came forward, caught hold of Darcy's arm.

The tall gambler shook them off.

'I can walk quite well without any help,' he said.

The two sailors took their hands away. But they kept close to Darcy as they escorted him to his cabin.

The one named Bull — his first name was Aloysious — was a big Irishman whom Darcy had known for many years. Before he shut and locked the door on the tall gambler he said:

'Don't worry, Darcy. Brunello may be a cold fish, but he's straight. An' everybody on the river knows you always give a man an even break.'

2

News of the Woman

Darcy Kane paced his small cabin until nightfall. From time to time he heard movements outside, so he figured there was a guard on him.

It wouldn't be Aloysious Bull or the big Irishman would have called out to his old friend by now. It must be the other man. The one called Macell. Darcy didn't know him. He was a surly-looking brute with the battered, formless face of an ex-pugilist.

Eventually the key turned in the lock. The door was opened and Darcy learned that his assumption had been correct. Macell looked in. He held a tray of food, a steaming mug of coffee.

Darcy took the tray from him, said: 'What's going on?'

'I don't know. Nobody's told me.'

Macell began to close the door again. 'Yell when you want me to take the tray back.' The door shut firmly. The key grated in the lock again.

Darcy forgot his puzzlement. He was very hungry so he attacked the meal.

What were they doing up there, holding a goddamned inquest? No doubt the dead man's four pards were screaming for blood. What was Fancy Jack doing?

Darcy rose. He hammered on the panels of the door. 'Hey, sailor, do you want this tray back?'

The key turned. The door was opened again. Wordlessly, the pug-faced sailor took the tray.

Darcy said: 'I left my hat upstairs by the table. I'm kind of attached to that hat. I'd like somebody to bring it to me.'

'Well, I can't get it for you. I've had orders not to move from this door. This cap'n's a tartar. If I move he'll have my skin. You'll have to wait 'till somebody else comes down.'

The door was closed, locked again.

Darcy sat down on his bunk, lit a cheroot.

He remembered that the last one he had lit had gone unsmoked. It probably still lay in the ashtray on the gaming-table. Since Darcy had lit that one a man had died, snuffed out more quickly than the hot ash of the cheroot could have been.

But he had asked for it. It had been self-defence.

The man had worn his Colt low-down, tied to his thigh by a whang-string, the way a regular Western gunfighter did, a professional. You didn't get a great amount of folks like him and his four pards this far South. But Darcy knew their type. It was a deadly type.

Yes, the man had been a gunfighter all right. He had had a fast, smooth draw. But it hadn't been fast enough. Darcy was as swift with a gun as he was with cards.

The man in the ten-gallon hat wasn't

the first man he had killed.

But surely! — and as Aloysious Bull had said — everybody on the river knew Darcy Kane ... Even Cap'n Brunello should know that Darcy Kane always gave the other man an even break.

★　★　★

The cabin was dark except for the glowing tip of the gambler's cheroot. Then he stubbed this out and he rose and lit the hanging lamp.

The key turned in the lock again and the door was opened.

This time it was Aloysious Bull and he had Darcy's hat, a black velvet slouch with a snakeskin band.

He moved into the cabin and closed the door behind him.

He spoke softly, quickly: 'I haven't got much time. Also, Macell out there has ears like a bat. Things ain't going too well, old friend. The only actual witnesses of the shooting are the dead

15

man's friends an' you know what they say. And now you're locked up out of harm's way Fancy Jack has swung around to their way . . . '

'I was afraid o' that,' said Darcy.

' . . . Yeh, an' Fancy Jack says you were cheating . . . '

'He's the one who was cheating.'

'I know it. But the Cap'n's pretty new to the river an' he's listening to them five of 'em. And there's a sixth.'

'A sixth?'

'That woman Fancy Jack brought on the boat with him. She was close by the table. She said she saw you draw first.'

'She couldn't have.'

At this juncture, the door was knocked. Macell's gruff voice called, 'What you doing in there, Al? I'm in charge of the prisoner.'

'I'll have to go,' said Aloysious quickly. 'Or I might be stopped coming here altogether. I'll get to you again as soon as I can.'

'All right. Thanks, Al.'

The Irishman took his leave. Darcy

sat on his bunk again. Absentmindedly, he put his slouch hat on his head.

God, he thought, I'd forgotten all about the woman.

Women were, you might say, a sort of a hobby with him. He couldn't help it if most of them went for him in a big way.

But he kept his women and business strictly apart. When he was on a gaming trip he forgot all about women. He disregarded the women on any boat, no matter how beautiful they were.

He would never have dreamed of taking a woman on a trip with him the way Fancy Jack did. Mixing business with pleasure! To Darcy that was a kind of sacrilege. It was almost as if that worm, Jack, needed a woman with him all the time to give him confidence. He fleeced the suckers. And his women fleeced him.

This present one was a good looking gal, you had to say that. Tall, taller than Jack. Dark, beautiful, voluptuous. She had ogled Darcy with her big black bedroom eyes. But he was on a business trip, and had his anti-female armour on.

He had disregarded her. He had known she was near the table — near her man — while the game went on. He would only have acknowledged her if she had got too close to the table, close enough to pass signals to Fancy Jack.

He had had that trick tried on him before. But she hadn't come that close, so, as far as Darcy was concerned, she hadn't been there at all. But she *had*! And now she was making him know she had. With the help of her little man she was sewing Darcy up in a bag and throwing him to the wolves.

Unless Brunello saw through her, saw through the whole thing!

He would like to see Brunello again. But not to push things. There was still plenty of time; this was a long trip. He had been in tighter spots than this one. He could wait, see what sort of a hand Lady Luck intended to deal him.

What was that filly's name? Fancy Jack's filly? He had almost forgotten it.

Something exotic!
Carmen, that was it.
Carmen.
He hunted through his baggage for his spare pack of cards and he began to play Patience.

3

The Escape

The night went on. Darcy Kane was immersed in his game to the exclusion of all else. He had long ago schooled himself to be like that. To be dispassionate, cool, single-minded.

The key turned in the lock and he looked up. The door opened. It was Aloysious Bull again.

The big Irishman halted in the centre of the cabin, his long hands dangling. He blinked in the light. His broad weatherbeaten face wore a grave expression.

'I've relieved Macell,' he said. 'He's out of the way now. Clip me on the jaw as hard as you can, Darcy, and then jump overboard. At this point of the river it's not far to the shore,' he jerked a thumb, 'that way.'

Darcy stood up.

'Hell, I can't run, Al. It'd be an admission of guilt. I appreciate you sticking your neck out for me, but . . . '

'I could tell 'em you jumped me, slugged me. They couldn't disprove that . . . '

'But I'd be a wanted man. I don't cheat, you know that. I killed that man in self-defence. He looked like a killer, wore his gun like a killer. He went for his gun first . . . '

'I know that without you telling me, even though I wasn't anywhere near when it happened. I know you. But the cap'n doesn't know you an' he's a stiffnecked an' bitter man — he's prejudiced. Fancy Jack an' the rest of 'em have got you sewn up. If you don't get out while you can, come St Louis you'll be in irons, you'll be lynch-mob meat. Those so-called cattle-buyers get off at St Louis. They aim to travel by road into Nebraska, or so they say. They'll want blood before they do. If you get any kind of trial at all it'll be a mighty quick one. You got to get away, Darcy. Folks soon forget. You could go West for a while . . . '

'If I go West it'll be to look for those four skunks,' said Darcy. 'Before I look for Fancy Jack and that woman of his . . . '

He shut up quickly then. As if ashamed of his passionate outburst, so foreign to his usual easy-going, nerveless nature.

'Fancy Jack is jealous of you,' Aloysious Bull told him. 'He'd like to get you off the river. An' if he can get your neck stretched at the same time that's fine by him. As for the woman — while Jack's on the upgrade, she's sticking by him. I tell you, Darcy, you've got to get moving.'

The tall gambler looked uncertain. For one of the few times in his adult life he didn't know what to do. 'Clip me on the chin,' said Aloysious. 'Come on. Quickly! Before somebody comes snoopin'. Clip me!'

'I can't do that, Al,' said Darcy

slowly. 'Not to you.'

'For Pete's sake!' exploded the Irishman 'Why not? If you don't clip me, they'll know I let you loose. Then I shall really be in trouble. They'll be stringing me up in your place.'

Aloysious then did quite a strange thing. He turned away from Darcy and lowered his bullet head. He spaced his feet apart, bent his knees.

'If you don't clip me, I'm going to charge. I'm going to ram my head up against that wall and knock myself out.'

'No . . . You might crack your skull. I couldn't let . . . '

'Clip me then! If you don't want me to see it, you can hit me on the back of the head with something.'

'I can't do that either . . . '

Darcy paused. He shrugged, smiled.

'Turn around,' he said.

Aloysious Bull straightened himself up. He turned slowly on his heels.

As he came to face Darcy, the tall gambler hit him full on the point of the jaw. It was a beautifully-placed blow.

The Irishman's eyes turned upwards blankly. He tottered like a felled tree.

Darcy caught him before he hit the floor. The huge dead weight almost brought them both down.

Darcy lowered his friend gently. 'Thank you, Al.' He smiled. 'I'll do the same for you some day.'

Now he had made his decision — a tough one though it had been — he moved fast. He stepped out into the empty passage, closed the door on the lighted room, the still figure. He locked the door behind him.

He made his way up on deck without seeing anybody. Then as he poised at the rail a dark figure came along the deck towards him.

Darcy leapt into the cold waters of the Mississippi. The waters closed over him, tried to pull him down. He struggled out of his coat.

He heard somebody shout, 'Man overboard.'

He began to swim strongly.

A rifle cracked back at the boat and a bullet spat in the water behind him. They had realized now who the 'man overboard' actually was.

Another bullet came a bit closer. And then the slugs fell behind and Darcy knew he was out of range. He looked ahead. A dark line of trees fringed the shore. There were no lights anywhere. This might have been a dead world.

A little later he crawled up the gravelly bank, dripping with water like a half-drowned rat. He found grass and he rolled over on it, gasping and shivering.

He sat up and began to beat at himself with hands and arms to try and warm himself up. The water of the river splashed from him like rain.

He had no coat, no gun, no food. Some money in his body-belt, though, protected and dry. His luck hadn't *completely* run out. Only almost!

He didn't know where he was.

Also he had left his favourite hat back there in the cabin. The hat that Aloysious had so kindly returned to him. Strangely enough, the loss of the hat seemed then to be the worst thing of all.

He hoped Aloysious would be all right.

He looked out across the river at the lights of the riverboat and he saw that they were stationary. He heard a voice — obviously Cap'n Brunello's — giving orders. He heard the rattle and splash of a boat being lowered. Then the sound of oars.

He rose and turned and began to make his way through the trees. They were dense. He had to plough his way through tangled undergrowth. But it was warmer here, protected from the wind. His wet clothes began to dry on him. He even began to sweat.

Suddenly he broke out into the open. Grass. A narrow road.

There was a glimmer of light over to the right of him. He crawled through a

26

wire fence and across a field planted with scrawny sugar-beet.

The light he had seen came from the window of a tumbledown farm. Another light glowed dimly from the door of a sagging-roofed barn beside it.

Darcy couldn't see anybody but from the barn came the sound of hammering. As if somebody was shoeing a horse. Walking softly on the pulpy ground Darcy crossed to the barn.

The whole place stank like a midden.

He moved into the barn.

The man dropped the horse's hoof, straightened up, his hammer in his hand.

The horse was a magnificent black stallion.

But the man was a scrawny, ragged, unshaven creature. A 'poor white'. The lowest form of human life in the South, lower even than a negro fieldhand who at least had his own friends and a measure of security.

These poor white families always had the scrub and barren land that was left over after the big landowners had grabbed everything else. They scrabbled bare sustenance from the earth. They lived like animals, keeping apart even from their own kind.

The man looked startled, shifty. The wet dishevelled Darcy must have looked quite a sight to him. The man stood with his mouth open, hunch-shouldered, gripping his hammer. He was inarticulate. He stood at bay like an animal.

Darcy said harshly, commandingly, 'I want a horse and a gun. A coat too. A slicker — anything to cover me up a bit better. I'll pay well.'

The other man's dull eyes lit up a bit at the mention of money. His lips yammered.

He said in a half-whine: 'That's the only hoss I can let you have, suh.'

He pointed to a broken stall in a shadowy corner of the barn. Darcy couldn't see the horse clearly but it looked like an ancient spavined brute.

'How about that one?' He pointed at

the black stallion.

'It don't belong to me, suh. I'm shoein' it for somebody else. Anyway, it's only got two shoes so far an' 'ud go lame on you 'fore you'd gone more'n a mile.'

The man was right, Darcy knew that. Besides he didn't have time to argue. His pursuers would probably have reached land now.

'Bring that one over then,' he said.

The man went over to the stall, brought forth the nag. A fugitive from a boneyard, a freak of a horse. 'She runs pretty good, suh,' whined the man.

'You sure this is the only other horse you've got?'

'Yes, suh. We're poor people. I don't know what we gonna do . . . '

'All right, all right. I'll take her. I want a gun, a coat.' Darcy opened his shirt, the top of his pants to get at his body belt. The other man had moved again, was getting down a moth-eaten blanket-coat from a nail in the wall. Darcy extracted a roll of greenbacks from his belt. The man turned and saw them and his eyes popped.

'Th-this is the warmest coat I got, suh,' he stammered. 'You're welcome to it . . . I shall have to go in the house for the gun. I've only got one. But I've got a rifle . . . '

'I'll take the gun.'

'Yes, suh . . . surely.'

Darcy began to peel bills from the roll.

The other man's eyes had widened again. But he wasn't looking at the money now, or at Darcy even. He was looking over Darcy's shoulder.

The tall gambler began to turn.

'Stay still, mister,' said a feminine voice. 'I got a rifle pointed at your spine.'

A female voice. But with a deadly, metallic ring. The woman meant what she said.

Darcy stayed put.

4

Yellow-haired Filly

He heard the woman move. Her slippered or moccasined feet made only a tiny snick-snick sound over the dirt and straw of the barn floor.

'Take the belt off and toss it to my pa,' the voice said.

A girl. Just a kid!

Darcy took off the body belt, tossed it. The man caught it, but only automatically: he was still bug-eyed.

'Put your hands up,' said the girl.

Darcy raised his hands.

'Now turn around slow an' easy.'

Darcy turned around and faced her. He got quite a surprise.

She was tall for a woman. A girl. Seventeen or eighteen maybe, not much more anyway. She was slim and shapely even in the skirt and baggy shirtwaist she wore. Her hair was long and wavy, reaching down to her shoulders, shining like golden corn in the dim light. Her face was a little drawn and pale but quite beautiful. Her eyes were large and blue, her lips full, red almost as if they had been painted. They stood out vividly in the pale face. She had small, high breasts. Her body was long and shapely, as were her bare brown legs. On her small feet were soft, scuffed moccasins.

'Lady,' Darcy said. 'All I wanted was a horse and a gun. You can't rob a man because he asks for help.'

The girl did not meet his eyes. But her face had taken on a hard and vicious look. She said:

'You're on the run. Anybody can see that.' She stood aside from the door, jerked the muzzle of the rifle. 'Go on then, run!'

'Give me my money back.'

'It'll do more good to pa and me than it will to you.'

Darcy began to move slowly towards

the door. He debated making a quick leap sideways, grabbing at her. But she handled that rifle like a professional and looked quite capable of using it too. She looked desperate — and hungry. Yeh, that was the word: *hungry*.

He had to get out of here. He hadn't much time. He said:

'All right. Take the money if you need it. But give me a horse an' gun.'

'A gun!' scoffed the girl.

She seemed to be beating herself into a kind of frenzy.

'We'd be fine suckers to give you a gun now wouldn't we'?' she demanded. 'An' we need the horse more than you do. Go on! On your way.'

Darcy had halted, was looking at her. She still would not meet his eyes. She said:

'Go on, before I shoot you where you stand.' Her voice had begun to crack. She was on the edge of hysteria. She's liable to shoot me out of sheer nervousness, thought Darcy. Hell, these people must be in a bad way.

But so was he. He certainly needed a horse.

But if he hung around here any longer he was liable to get shot anyway. By the girl. Or by somebody from the river boat. He started to move again.

He went through the door. He heard the girl following him. The sibilant round of her moccasins in the dirt and straw.

As he crossed the filthy yard he looked back. She was limmed against the glow at the barn door. She had the rifle pointed straight at him.

She began to walk out after him.

'Keep going,' she said. 'Take the road.'

When he reached the road she was still behind him, silhouetted in the beet field. Darcy was shivering with cold. He began to run. He turned a bend of the road and the girl was lost to his view.

★ ★ ★

The trees loomed at the side of him. The men from the boat would be coming through there. Darcy moved into the trees, lost himself in the deep gloom. Then he paused and listened. He could hear no sound.

He figured the people in the boat would come ashore at about the same spot as he had, that they would come out in the road near the farm. That is if they didn't spread out. They were just sailors though, not trained hunters. He didn't think they would spread out.

He had been tempted to keep moving, get as far ahead as he possibly could. They'd have to give up the chase pretty quickly and go back to the riverboat, which was supposed to run a schedule. Then he would be free to do what he wanted to do, free to ultimately clear himself.

But stumbling through the dark night, wet and cold and penniless: that wasn't being free. Chivvied by a stripling of a girl with a rifle, chased away like a whipped cur with its tail between its legs: that wasn't being free either.

He shook himself angrily. He began to move through the trees softly and carefully, going roughly parallel with the route he had taken in the first place. Going back towards the river, towards danger.

He paused from time to time and listened. And then finally he heard his pursuers. They were pretty close. He saw the low bough of a tree and he reached up and grasped it. He levered himself up into the tree, feeling foolish, like a goddamned monkey. He hid himself in the foliage.

He heard them pass, talking in low voices. They seemed to be all together in a bunch.

Darcy waited till they had passed, until he was quite sure there was nobody else. Then he came down from his tree and followed.

He went carefully, listening all the time.

When he reached the edge of the trees they were in the road. He crouched, watching. There were five of them, all crew-men as far as Darcy could see. Quite naturally none of them thought of looking behind them. And even if they had they couldn't have spotted their quarry in the deep gloom.

One of them pointed at the light of the farm. Then they all crawled beneath the fence wire and set out across the field of sugar beets.

They weren't used to hunting men. Or to any other kind of hunting for that matter. If they had been, a couple of them would have stayed behind, watched the road.

It didn't take them long to find out what they wanted at the farm.

I bet that filly didn't tell 'em about the money, thought Darcy sardonically.

He saw them coming back. They went along the road. They seemed to be arguing. Two of them wanted to give up the hunt, go back to the boat. They were for the moment, overruled. The whole bunch went on along the road.

Keeping in cover of the trees, Darcy tailed them.

He was warmer now. He was even beginning to enjoy himself.

★   ★   ★

After they had gone about a mile along the road without spotting their quarry, the bunch began to argue among themselves again. Then finally they turned about and one of them said, 'I vote we go back along the road till we get by the farm, then go into the trees. We don't want to get lost.'

There seemed to be sense in this and they all complied. Darcy turned about also, kept pace with them once more. Then when they turned into the trees, he sank into the underbrush and they went right past him. It was as easy as that.

They were busy chewing the fat

again. If he had stood up straight, motionless, they would probably have walked round him, mistaking him for a tree.

He waited until their voices had died away in the distance, then he moved on to the road again, across it, through the wire.

He cut diagonally across the beet-field now. He made a detour in order to approach the farm from the back. There was no light in the barn, so the man had evidently finished shoeing the black stallion.

There was a light in the back of the farmhouse. The window was uncurtained. Darcy catfooted up there and looked in.

The kitchen was sparsely-furnished. The man and his daughter sat at the large deal table. Darcy's body-belt lay on the table-top and the money was spread out. The man and the girl were counting it. They were absorbed in their task, their heads downcast, their faces tense, avaricious, almost horrible.

Darcy spotted the rifle. It was leaned against the end of the table nearest the door. It was out of reach of both the girl and the old man.

5

Turnabout

Darcy moved to the door. He tried the latch and it gave. He flung the door wide, leapt through it.

The girl gave a little cry.

She half-rose. But by then Darcy had the rifle in his hand, levelled at both of them. The old man sat where he was, stared as if he couldn't believe his eyes. His mouth hung open.

'Sit down, honey,' said Darcy to the girl.

She sat down slowly like a moving doll. Her blue eyes were enormous in the beautiful white face.

Darcy held the rifle in the crook of his arm. He picked the body belt up from the table. He scooped the money towards him.

The old man's lips yammered. His

brown teeth made a clacking sound, but no words came. The girl sat still and cold and white as if she was made of ice.

Darcy said: 'Did you finish shoeing the black, Pop?'

The man made a sound in his throat. He nodded his head. He looked scared to death.

'I'm taking him,' said Darcy.

He hung the belt over his shoulder. He crammed some of the money roughly into his pants-pocket, left the rest on the table.

'That's for the horse. I guess he's worth that much. I'm taking the rifle too.'

He backed a little, threw quick glances around him. He saw an old black coat on a nail near the window. He crossed to it, took it down.

'I'll take this too.'

A door creaked. Darcy swivelled a little, his lips drawn back from his teeth.

'It's only the children,' cried the girl.

The leaning middle door had opened.

Two pale, peaked faces looked in.

'Come in, kids,' Darcy said gently. 'Shut the door behind you.'

Silently, like mice, they did as they were told. They were alike. They might have been twins. Their threadbare nightdresses reached down to their feet. They stood staring at Darcy without fear in their large blue eyes. They both had yellow curly hair, one wearing it long, the other short. They were probably boy and girl.

Their sister, the elder girl, was looking at Darcy accusingly, with hate. She wasn't scared either. Despite his anger at the way she had treated him, he couldn't help but admire her guts.

He felt compelled to say, 'You didn't think I'd come back did you?'

'Get out of here,' she said from between set teeth.

It was like the hissing of a beautiful snake.

His daughter's fearlessness seemed to have given the old man some courage at last. He said:

'The horse — the black horse — he isn't mine . . . '

'All right. I'll send him back when I get a chance. I'm no horse-thief . . . Take the money.'

With trembling hands the man reached out and raked the bills towards him.

Darcy said:

'If you'd played it straight from the first I'd have been away now on that old nag you offered me. An' in the long run you'd be a sight better off.'

'We don't dicker with killers,' spat the girl. 'The men off the riverboat have been here. They told us about you.'

'You were ready to be a killer yourself a while ago. And with a lot less justification, believe me.'

'Scum,' she spat. 'Filthy river scum!'

She was working herself up into a rage again.

'Cut it!' barked Darcy.

She shut up.

'On your feet,' he said.

Slowly, she rose to her feet. There was uncertainty in her eyes now.

'Come here,' said Darcy. 'Quickly, I haven't got all night.'

She came round the table and towards him. He reached out with his free hand and grabbed her.

He drew her quickly to him and kissed her brutally on the lips.

She struggled at first. She even tried to grab the rifle. But then her body became limp, her lips soft, compliant.

He let her go.

'You don't belong in a rat-trap like this, honey,' he said. 'I'd like to take you with me but I can't. Maybe I'll get a chance to come back some day and then you'll hear the truth of this whole thing.'

She did not go back to her seat, but just stood there. She wasn't looking at him now. Her head was downcast. Her golden hair shone in the light of the hanging hurricane lantern. He had an idea she was listening though, listening intently.

She did not say anything.

Darcy went on: 'I'm going over to the barn to get the horse. Don't nobody try and follow me. Don't forget I've got the rifle.'

He walked out quickly, closing the door behind him. The black stallion was standing docilely in a stall. There was a small blanket over his back but Darcy could not see any saddle. He would have to ride him bareback.

The horse rolled its eyes at him as he approached. He spoke to it gently, softly, and it became quiet.

He led it from the stall, talking to it and gentling it all the time. He put his bodybelt on quickly. He vaulted on to the horse's back, gripped the smooth flanks with his knees.

The horse shied a bit at first but soon settled down. Holding the rifle in the crook of his arm, Darcy rode the horse at a canter from the barn. Nothing moved near the farmhouse.

There in the barn the first time the old man said he had a gun in the house, reflected Darcy. Another gun — not the rifle.

Would they try to use it? He didn't want to start shooting if he could help it, specially with those kids there.

But he rode the horse across the field to the road and nothing happened. Then he clung to the horse's mane as best he could while holding the rifle at the same time.

He suddenly realized he hadn't brought the coat away with him, the black coat he had taken from the wall.

That poor white filly had had an effect on him all right. Her fearlessness had almost thrown him off-balance. She had had a greater effect on him than any swell society frail in New Orleans or St Louis.

The horse was a powerful beast. He moved smoothly too, so that the going wasn't quite as rough as it might have been to a saddleless man.

They sped on through the night.

6

House in St Louis

At a little town a few miles away from the farm Darcy rode the horse into a livery-stable that was open late. A fat unshaven man shuffled to meet him, stared at this big man, hatless, coatless, damp, bedraggled.

Darcy grinned at him. 'We fell in the river, me an' my friend here.' He patted the horse. 'My saddle was loose. I lost it. Have you an old one you can sell me? An' maybe a coat to keep out the cold?'

Darcy hoped the black stallion wasn't known in this town. But the fat man seemed to accept Darcy's explanation, which was quite a logical one after all. His little eyes twinkled with amusement.

'We got lost,' said Darcy. 'I don't ride

as much as I used to.' He patted the horse again. 'I hadn't ridden him for ages and I guess he was getting back at me.'

As if in answer, the stallion snorted and tossed his head.

'He's a lovely beast,' said the fat man, obviously a lover of good horseflesh.

Darcy dismounted. He took the blanket from the horse's back, took a handful of dry straw from the floor and began to rub him down. The fat man moved into the shadows in back of the bar, returned with a battered but serviceable saddle and a scuffed black-leather coat.

They made a deal to suit them both and, saddled-up adequately now, Darcy went on his way. Along the road a signpost gave him a clue and by daylight he was well on the way to his first destination.

This he reached later in the day.
St Louis.

★   ★   ★

At that time St Louis was a notorious river town. Sprawling, blustering, colourful, rather like a fast woman down on her luck but still with traces of her old beauty. It was a friendly town if you didn't pry too much into the other feller's private business.

If a man wanted to get lost here, he could easily do so if he knew the ropes. And Darcy Kane knew the ropes all right.

He was known on the water-front, might get spotted there. So he kept away from it.

He knew he had beaten the riverboat to its call here. And here, or so Aloysious Bull had told him, the four so-called cattle-buyers would disembark and make their way by road into Nebraska.

Darcy knew also that Fancy Jack and Carmen had planned to disembark here and set up a game for a while in St Louis, which was a hotbed of gambling. Would Fancy Jack still do this? If so, there was maybe a chance for Darcy to get hold of him — and that lying filly, Carmen — and make them tell the truth to Captain Brunello.

Darcy went first to a house at the edge of town. A two-storey frame building discreetly surrounded by juniper trees. A porch with subdued lighting which burned all night. By daytime as horse and rider approached, it might have been a house of the dead. But he knew that by night, all through the night, it would be bursting at the seams with music and laughter, the shouts of men and women enjoying themselves. It was fun-palace, dance-hall, gambling-house and saloon all rolled into one and was kept by an elderly couple called Sadie and Matt, a tough pair who stood no nonsense from anybody.

And Sadie and Matt were very old and valued friends of Darcy Kane's.

In fact, he had worked as a house-man running their gambling-rooms for them for about six months before the lure of the river started him on travelling again.

They were hardheaded business people, were Sadie and Matt. They could be quite ruthless. But they were straighter than most people who ran any kind of joint. Like Darcy they always gave folks an even break, they went by how the chips fell, they didn't judge others and didn't expect to be judged. They had sympathy for the underdog and many a comfortable-living cuss had to thank them for the stake that had got him started.

Darcy went round to the back of the house. It was a damp, dark morning with a grey mist. It couldn't have been better for Darcy's purpose. He hardly saw anybody as he came in on the back road and approached the house.

The back curtains were closed and in a ground floor window a light glowed. This was a huge kitchen, Darcy knew. The place where Sadie spent most of her days. She had shut the dark morning out and was probably sitting in the lamplight making up her accounts or crocheting or maybe reading a book slowly with much moving of her lips.

And Matt, if he wasn't out getting provisions, would be out front, helping to get the place tidy for the evening, superintending the roustabouts and making sure they did not take too much liquor out with them.

Darcy tapped on the window boldly.

He heard Sadie's rocking-chair creak as she rose. He heard her footsteps scuttling. She moved very lightly and swiftly, though she was a big elderly woman.

He heard the window open a little. But the curtains did not open.

Sadie's voice said: 'Who are you? Speak up quick. I've got a shotgun here an' I ain't too shy to use it'

'It's me, Sadie. Darcy Kane.'

'Darcy!'

The curtains were parted then and the broad pugnacious face looked out at him from beneath its thick and glorious crown of snow-white hair.

'Why'n't you come to the door, boy?'

'I know you always keep it locked. I'll go there now.' He moved along to the back door. He heard the bolts being drawn, the chain clinking. There was plenty of money in this place most of the time and Sadie and Matt took no foolish chances.

The door was opened. Darcy stepped inside and the big woman closed it behind him.

'Lemme put up the fortifications again,' she said. Bolts shooting home, chain clanking into place. Then Sadie turned to face Darcy.

'God, boy,' she said, 'What you been doin' to yourself? You look awful.'

'It's kind of a long story.'

'You just got off a boat?'

'No, I came across country by horseback.'

Sadie looked at him shrewdly, 'You on the run from somethin', boy?'

'Yes, I am. I'll tell you about it . . . '

'Save it. Let's get you a change of

clothes and some chow first. You want to wash up?'

'My horse's outside. I'd like to see to him first.'

'Hell, one of the boys'll do that for you!'

'I'd rather do it myself, Sadie.'

The woman shrugged her massive shoulders.

'Drat you,' she said as she bent to the door again.

'Let me do that,' said Darcy and he took her place.

'I'll get a tub ready for you,' said Sadie.

But she locked the door behind him again before doing this.

Darcy took the black stallion to the stable in the back of the house. He rubbed him down, gave him some oats. He had grown attached to this magnificent beast. The horse seemed to have taken to him too, nuzzling him playfully now.

Darcy knew, however, that he'd have to figure some way to get the beast back to its owner. He had probably already got the stigma of 'horse-thief' added to his other crimes. But at least he'd try to put this right first of all.

*   *   *

He turned quickly as he heard somebody approaching. He had left his rifle back in the house. He would have to get another hand-gun as soon as possible. His shoulder-holster hung damply, limply, uselessly.

'Darcy,' a voice called and the tall gambler almost sighed aloud with relief.

'Here,' he answered.

Big Matt entered the stable. His cropped hair was grey. His face was deeply seamed, lantern-jawed, the face of a man who had seen much through the long years. His eyes were deepset and keen beneath thick startlingly-black eyebrows. He was big; taller than his wife but not so broad. 'Big Matt' some folks called him.

Sadie and Matt were both Texans but they had been in this part of the South since their younger days when they first got hitched. Sadie had been a dance-hall girl, Matt a gambler like Darcy.

They liked each other fine, this elderly man and the young one. In Darcy maybe, Matt saw himself when young though he had never had Darcy's polish and education, had never been able to make the pasteboards talk quite the way Darcy did or had been so handy with a gun.

He did not ask the younger man any questions right then but walked companionably back to the house with him.

Sadie had a steaming tub ready in the little private bathhouse that led off from the kitchen. She had clean clothes laid out that belonged to her husband. They would fit Darcy all right for he was a big man too, though leaner and less stooped than Matt.

There were shaving utensils there too and Darcy gave himself a complete going-over. When he got back into the

57

kitchen he was glowing like a new pin.

Sadie had a hot meal ready for him. Steak and french fries and onions. Apple pie with maple syrup and whipped cream. Coffee with brandy. A couple of Darcy's favourite cheroots.

While the tall gambler was indulging himself Matt said: 'I'll go back out front. It ain't safe to leave some of those ginks on their own for long. Call me when you feel like a chinwag.'

'Sure, Matt.'

Sadie seated herself in her rocking chair again. She picked up her steel-rimmed spectacles and perched them on her fleshy nose. She was reading a large leatherbound book which, Darcy saw, was *Gulliver's Travels*.

She ran her fingers along the lines, forming the words with her lips.

She did not bother the young man, let him eat in peace, drink, lean back with a satisfied sigh, light a cheroot.

'That was fine, Sadie,' he said. 'Mighty fine. You always were the best cook along the river.'

'Matt's allus been a big eater,' said Sadie. 'Always appreciated his food.'

'Him and me both,' said Darcy.

He hesitated. Then he said: 'Would you call Matt, Sadie honey? I want to tell you both why I'm here, what happened.'

'Sure, Darcy.'

Sadie went over to the communicating door, opened it, yelled for her husband in the raucous penetrating voice she used in her louder moments. Many a troublemaker had cringed as Sadie's clarion call fell about his ears. And more than that fell too if he didn't back down quickly.

Matt came a-running.

Slowly, not missing anything out, Darcy told his two old friends the whole story of what he was compelled to term sardonically as his 'downfall'.

They heard him out without comment. They had heard many such stories, some of them a complete pack of lies. But it was evident that they believed every word of this one. They knew Darcy too well . . . at times he had been like a son to them.

He could be ruthless for these were ruthless times and his was a dangerous profession. He could and had killed more than once, they knew that. But they knew that he lived by a code, if only the code of the best of professional gamblers. A code, in fact, that many a businessman, looking down on the lawless breed as 'scum', might have done well to emulate.

Sadie and Matt knew that Darcy would not cheat and would not kill anybody in cold blood.

Matt said: 'You're welcome to hide out here and rest up for as long as you like, son. An' I'll give you any help I can to straighten this thing out, you know that.'

And Sadie who, like most women, thought in personalities, said viciously:

'That Fancy Jack. There's a snake for you. I allus did hate his insides.'

Darcy had a thoughtful look on his face. 'Does Fancy Jack still come here?'

'Sometimes.'

'I hope he doesn't figure out that I might be here and set the wolves on us. I don't want you to get mixed up in . . .'

'Hell!' exploded Matt. 'What are friends for? Let these people come if they hafta. We'll work somp'n out.'

Sadie spoke up again, but quietly now. Her voice was soft and deadly.

'If Fancy Jack does come here mebbe that'd be the chance to grab him, make him tell the truth.'

Then all three of them were silent as they chewed over this possibility in their minds.

The light was getting better. The mist drifted away. A pale, damp-looking sun came out.

Sadie was able to turn out the lamp and draw back the curtains and let the daylight in.

7

Thieves' Quartet — Plus Two

Fancy Jack always took the line of least resistance. He knew that Darcy Kane hadn't shot the 'cattle-buyer' in cold blood, but only in self-defence. Darcy had been a faster gun, that was all.

He knew that Darcy had not cheated. He himself had been the only cheat at that table. He knew that Darcy had suspected this but, because Darcy was winning, he hadn't called Jack down.

He should've called Jack down. His easy-going Quixotry had almost lost him his freedom or his life. It had already lost him his good name. But Fancy Jack just did not think about Darcy's fate in this way. He only had thoughts for his own welfare and that of his own plump soft carcass.

He had gone along with the four

Westerners and what they said because he was too scared to do anything else. He knew killers when he saw them. Darcy Kane was a killer too. But Darcy was on the run and the four Westerners were still menacingly present.

Darcy had evaded the law. But Fancy Jack knew that the four friends of the now-defunct man in the ten-gallon hat would still get the tall gambler if they had the chance. Fancy Jack realized that it would be best for him if Darcy were dead and the four hardcases were back West where they belonged.

As for Carmen, Jack's girl: she went along with Jack and what Jack said because at the time Jack was her 'protector' and that was how it had to be. She'd stick by Jack until something better came along.

The riverboat reached St Louis. By this time the body of the man in the ten-gallon hat — whose name was Simmons — was incarcerated in a plain wooden coffin. Simmons was getting ripe, so there would have to be a short sharp service in St Louis after the local law had viewed the cadaver and received Cap'n Brunello's report about the escaped gambler-killer.

All this was done. The four Westerners kept close to the other witnesses. Fancy Jack and his woman kept talking their heads off, perjuring themselves a mile a minute, getting in deeper all the time.

Simmons and his four pardners had been a well-knit team. Simmons had been the leader by virtue of his faster gun-hand, his rock-hard fists, his vicious temper. But his temper had finally brought about his downfall, his gunhand hadn't been fast enough.

The others had missed him for a while. But they were a *team*, there was no gainsaying that, and they began to tell themselves, individually and collectively, that they could do without Simmons.

Also — and this made Simmons' death right — the proceeds for their last job would now be split four ways instead of five.

On the other hand, Simmons' death must be avenged. That was the code. And it was a code that had its practical aspects too. The incident on the boat had drawn much undue attention to the four men. Attention that was very unwelcome to them. Darcy Kane had many friends on the river and as long as he was loose and able to talk attention would still be drawn to the four men.

They had planned to leave St Louis after landing and make their way on up West. But they had an idea that Kane and maybe a few of his friends might be on their tails.

So they had to get Kane. And Fancy Jack and his woman were the decoy ducks that might help to bring this about. So they kept close to Jack. To Jack who knew who Kane's friends were, who knew where Kane might choose to hide until he felt it was time to act.

And Kane was of the breed who

would act sooner or later, the four hardcases made no mistake about that. Kane was the kind that made a very bad enemy.

Even so the four of them were still divided about what actual policy to follow in the case of Kane. For they were hunted men too. They had been pretty sure of having thrown their hunters off long since. But there was no knowing but that if they stayed too long in the South the hunters might pick up the scent again. And then there was the money. They were humping the money around with them.

They were indeed Westerners, none of whom had been far into the South before. They had all been cowhands at one time or another, but never 'cattle-buyers'. They had stuck up a Southern bank and a cashier had been killed.

They had escaped unscathed. Everything would have been rosy if Simmons hadn't insisted on trying his luck on the riverboat.

Well, Simmons had paid for that.

On the other hand, although they wouldn't admit it to each other they were still a bit lost without the big man's leadership. If he hadn't gotten himself killed there wouldn't be any problem, for his killing had been the crux of that. But still they didn't quite know what to do, and they argued about this.

★   ★   ★

If there was any leader at all among them now it was Grey Burnette. He was lithe and lean, hatchet-featured and had sandy hair and the pale flat eyes of an utterly consciousless killer.

He was fast with a gun and had an itchy trigger-finger. It was he who had shot the cashier during the bank job. A young man who had been quite harmless but who had moved a bit too abruptly for the snakish Greg's peace of mind.

Burnette had always been jealous of

Simmons. Had it ever come to a stand-up gunfight between the two of them. there was no guessing who would have been the victor. But Simmons had been a bull of a man, fast with fists and mouth and he had always over-ridden the weaker Burnette.

Strangely enough, it was Burnette now who plumped for avenging Simmons' death. They had to shut Kane's mouth for good, he said, do it themselves. They'd have no peace until they did. For even if the law got Kane, that wouldn't be the end of it! There would be a trial and Burnette and his friends would have to appear. Then somebody might recognize them and put two and two together and make an ominous four. And then Kane wouldn't be the only one who'd end swinging on a rope.

No, they had to get Kane quickly and secretly. Fancy Jack would lead them to him, Burnette said. Or, alternatively, Kane would come looking for Jack, or for all of them.

. . . And afterwards Jack and his woman would have to be gotten rid of too, before the boys could become free as birds and light out for the West.

Kill, kill, *kill*: that was the only kind of language Greg Burnette understood. Also, though he didn't admit this to his pards, he would like to try out that Kane.

He had wanted to try out Simmons some day, had known that inevitably that day would come. But the chance had been taken away from him. Somebody else had tried Simmons, had taken Simmons. And now Burnette would like to try that somebody else.

The need to try Kane was beginning to eat at his guts like some kind of disease.

Even this would have to be done secretly, however, he had to agree with his friends on this.

But still there was friction.

Yellow-faced, squint-eyed Bat McGee had gone along with Burnette all the time. And now poker-faced Cherokee

Pete was coming round to their way of thinking too.

But little rat-faced Sam Konacky still held out. He wanted to light out for the West right away and leave all this behind them. Let the local authorities catch Darcy Kane.

He and the rest of the boys could hide out awhile up West if need be. He hated the South and the sooner they got out of it the better he'd feel.

He had been watching Fancy Jack and the girl. And now Cherokee Pete took over that chore while Burnette and the squint-eyed McGee tried their persuasive powers on Konacky.

If truth was told, now that the blustering Simmons was no longer here to keep them together, each of these four men was playing his cards very close to his chest.

Even Cherokee Pete had an ulterior motive for staying around here to see which way the cat jumped.

Had he put this motive into words, told his pards of it they would have screamed with lewd laughter. Pete was pretty inarticulate most of the time anyway.

His greatest passion, next to money, was women.

He was a well-built, darkly handsome man with a classic cast of features, raven-black hair and dark liquid eyes. His nickname 'Cherokee' was supposed to have been given him because he came from that place. But some folks said the name fitted him because his mother had been a squaw.

Cherokee Pete preferred to be called by his real name rather than its prefix. He didn't like being called half-Indian. He had killed two men at least because they made snide remarks about his past and his family.

Still, half-Indian or not, women went for him all right.

And now he desired Fancy Jack's woman, Carmen . . .

8

The Watcher

Don't get too close to Jack and the woman, Burnette had said, Kane might have friends hunting for us. We don't want to start a shindig in a public place. When we get him we want it quiet.

I don't want it quiet and quick and easy, he might have said, *me*, Greg Burnette, gunfighter *par excellence*. I've got to try this man, I've *got to*!

If Kane approaches Fancy Jack he'll probably do it alone and quietly, Burnette said. He might even grab the woman alone, force her to say she had lied. Watch them, Burnette said, they'll lead us to Kane, if anybody can.

So Cherokee Pete watched them, tailed them. He knew the small obscure grog-shop where he could find the others if he needed them.

The whole thing wasn't much of a plan but Pete, whose handsome head was full of everything but brains, didn't realize that. He didn't realize that if Simmons had been alive to plan this deal he would have done things differently.

Simmons had been the brains of the outfit as well as the brawn. Burnette was the next best thing. But Burnette was like a rabid dog. He would kill for the sake of killing and that was something that Simmons — unless he completely lost his temper — would never do.

But Cherokee Pete did not worry his handsome head about these things. He watched the tubby gambler strutting like a peacock. And he wanted the gambler's woman.

She was tall, dark, long-legged, high-breasted, voluptuously shapely. She was very lovely. Cherokee Pete went very big for such a woman, for this particular woman.

He wanted to stamp on the little

plump gambler, squash him like a bug. Such a little worm should not have such a woman.

But Pete was utterly amoral and cynical and he had no illusions. He knew Carmen stuck to Jack because at the moment Jack was in the chips. But right now Pete himself was probably even more in the chips, so there was no problem there. Also Carmen had given Pete more than one lingering glance from under her long black lashes and the handsome half-breed knew she would not be hard to win over, particularly if he crackled some of the long green near her shell-like ears.

Maybe it would be best to get Fancy Jack out of the way first, however, and avoid complications. Pete was handier with a knife than he was with a gun. He was not a pathological killer like Greg Burnette but, even so, he held life very cheaply and would kill on any justification.

His want of this woman, Carmen, was like a fire in his blood and he was quite willing to stick a knife between a fat, useless little gambler's ribs to get her. Whether the fire would last, was worth killing for, Pete didn't know. He didn't even think about this aspect. He could only figure out one thing at a time, could only wait his opportunity.

It came sooner than he expected.

He saw Darcy Kane again sooner than he expected. It was as if these two had been moving irrevocably towards each other. Like ships they would pass in the night but the actual head-on-clash would not come until much later.

As they passed, however, drew nearer, then further away as if in some abortive mating dance, other people would suffer first.

★   ★   ★

It was night again.

As Darcy Kane sat in the kitchen of Matt and Sadie's place he could hear the sounds of revelry out front. They got wilder and louder by the minute.

There would be some good games going Darcy knew. A man could sit in a sort of oasis with a few men of like kind and try his hand and his luck as the revelry swirled around him. But he could feel he belonged to the revelry too, was part of this blustering night-life.

Darcy wanted to be out there with the rest of them. With the poker-faced men and their hooded eyes, with the loud fancy women, and the soft ones too, with the dancing girls and roustabouts and businessmen and rummies and pimps and gunfighters and crooks. They were his world and he loved them and judged them not. He didn't want to skulk in a kitchen like a scared rabbit. He wanted to be out there with the rest of them, the rabbits and the wolves . . .

But there were two people to whom he owed a lot, two people he was more fond of maybe than any other two people in the world. And to go out front now would be jeopardizing them as well as himself.

So he stayed put.

★ ★ ★

Until Matt came in and said: 'He's here. That little worm, Fancy Jack. Seems to be alone too — except for his woman o' course.'

'What are they doing?'

'Jes drinkin' so far. Seems to me they're both gulping it down as if they want to get themselves well an' truly soused. I can't figure what they're doing here. Surely Fancy Jack ain't crazy enough to come a-looking for you.'

'No, he mightn't even guess I'm here. Fancy Jack wasn't around when I was house-man here, you may remember, Matt. As a matter of fact I think he was in jail.'

'Hmm, yeh, I remember that stretch Jack did — something to do with complicity in a gold-brick swindle. Yeh, maybe he doesn't know we're good

77

friends. Maybe he figures you're not likely to be near a public place like this but laying low in some hideout.'

'That's what he'd do.'

'It is.'

'Yeh, that's so,' said Darcy. 'I wish I could get the little skunk alone.'

'I could get him in here on some pretext.'

'No, I won't have you sticking your neck out any more, Matt. I have to be adamant about that now, old friend . . . Besides, there's the girl. It wouldn't be wise to leave her on her own. Apart from the fact that I need her testimony, too. You'd have to think up something pretty plausible to get 'em both out here . . . '

Darcy broke off, a thoughtful look on his face. Then he said:

'But if you could get 'em out back some place, in the stables or thereabouts maybe, where I could tackle them . . . '

He paused again, his head on one side. The two men looked at each other owlishly, both of them exploring possibilities in their minds.

'Has Jack got a horse in the stables?'

'I don't think he's got a horse at all if it comes to that.'

'No, of course not, he doesn't ride if he can help it. The fat worm doesn't look good in the saddle.'

'In any case,' said Matt. 'Only the regulars are allowed in the stables. Casual callers hitch their nags out front.'

'Yeh, yeh, of course.' Darcy smote his brow. 'Hell, what's the matter with my think-box tonight.'

'I'll keep an eye on 'em anyway,' said Matt. 'The way they're both going on I'll soon be able to roll 'em out back like goddamned barrels. Though Jack's new woman is the nicest barrel I've ever seen an' I've seen some barrels in my life.'

The conversation seemed to be lapsing into a form of repartee.

Then Darcy said: 'We've been thinking on the lines of luring Fancy Jack outside. Why not try it on the woman first. It might be quite easy. It's worth trying anyway.'

'What do you suggest?'

'Tell her there's a man wants to see her out back. Tell her it's an old friend. If the girl falls for it, I figure Jack will creep along to take a look at his rival.'

'I'll try,' said Matt. 'I'll lead her out there . . . '

'But don't stay. I don't want you mixed up in this.'

'All right, Darcy.'

'Lend me a gun, Matt. I shouldn't use it unless I have to.'

'All right, son. But don't go an' get yourself shot up. Remember that those four other ginks are lurking about some place.'

9

The Decoy Duck

Cherokee Pete took a small table in an unobtrusive corner from where he could keep an eye on the bar.

Fancy Jack and Carmen seemed to have laid claim to a certain section of the bar and they stayed there. They seemed to be knocking back quite a lot of the stuff. That filly sure can drink, thought Pete. He lost sight of them from time to time as other folks clustered behind them, clamoured for drinks. But had they moved away from the bar he would have spotted them.

Pete took a few drinks himself. He began to get bored. A painted woman sidled over and sat in the empty chair on the other side of his table. She was getting long in the tooth and her washed-out blue eyes were filled with an abysmal tiredness.

'You look kinda lonely, honey,' she said. 'Away up in a corner like this.'

Pete looked at her with disgust. 'I sat here 'cos I want to be lonely,' he said. 'Go peddle your pots some place else.'

'Don't be like that, honey.'

'Take a walk I said.' There was latent savagery in the handsome man's voice. His mahogany poker-face was still expressionless but his velvety eyes had a terrible look in them.

The woman's face went chalky beneath its paint. Without a word she got up and moved quickly away.

Then Pete was able to fix his eyes on that other woman again, the one he wanted. There was nobody in the way for the moment and he could see her clearly.

She was laughing at something, throwing her head back so that he could see the flawless arched column of her throat. Her dark glossy hair was tossed as her whole body shook with laughter. She was like a wild thing and

Pete thought he would like to tame her, tame her good.

His blood boiled when he saw Fancy Jack slide his arm around the slim waist. He forgot momentarily that she was the little gambler's woman, had been his woman on the boat and before that. He only saw them now and thought to himself that he couldn't let her stay with Jack any longer, not one night, not one hour more.

He began to rise to his feet. He didn't rightly know what he planned to do. Ask her to dance maybe: there were plenty of men and gels dancing. Ask her to have a drink maybe; or tell them both that Greg Burnette wanted to see 'em, then get rid of Fancy Jack somehow . . .

But then, as Pete was half on his feet he stopped. Somebody else had approached Carmen and Jack, was talking to them.

Cherokee Pete recognized the proprietor of this place, the tough-looking elderly man they called Big Matt. He seemed to be talking to the girl more than the man. Fancy Jack had taken his arm away from the girl's waist and seemed to be looking on suspiciously.

Cherokee Pete sat down slowly. He watched and waited.

The girl seemed to be questioning the big man. Then finally she nodded and the big man led the way, across the floor, cutting through the folks, some of whom greeted him, slapped his shoulder, joshed him about his fair companion. He led the girl through a side door, the door closing behind them. Cherokee Pete rose again, then paused once more, for Fancy Jack had started to follow the big man and the girl.

So Pete waited just a mite longer. And then he began to follow Jack.

He found himself outside. Jack was moving ahead of him along the side of the building. And then, after a pause, turning the corner and passing out of sight behind the house.

Pete reached the corner too and

peered around it. He looked out on the back of the house, an unfamiliar house to him. The big man had disappeared and Carmen was walking over to some outbuildings, stables probably, in which a light glowed dimly.

Fancy Jack followed her. She had not spotted him. Despite his fatness, he moved pretty lightly and swiftly. The girl went into the stable.

Then, after a bit, Jack followed her.

⋆　⋆　⋆

Darcy Kane stood in the shadows of the barn. In his fist he held the gun Big Matt had lent him. He said: 'Over here, honey, and make it fast. I wouldn't want to shoot a lovely lady like you.'

The girl gave a little cry, her hand flying to her throat. She looked towards the shadows and Darcy stepped a little way out of them and into the edge of light.

'You!' she gasped.

'Yes, me. Come on. Easy now.' He

jerked the muzzle of the gun.

Like an automaton she walked over to him.

'Stay there,' he said. 'Keep still and quiet.'

He went past her and over to the door. He stood beside the door.

The lurking Jack almost ran into him.

'Join the party, Jack,' said Darcy.

Jack stopped dead. His mouth shot open in terror. He acted automatically, instinctively. He turned about, began to walk, seemed on the point of running. A brave man wouldn't have been so foolish. Jack was an arrant coward. He acted very foolhardy.

'Not another step, Jack,' barked Darcy, 'or, by Jehosophat, I'll blow a hole in your spine.'

The words penetrated to the plump gambler's senses and he stopped dead. Darcy moved out into the doorway.

'Turn around and come back here,' he said.

Jack turned about slowly. He walked back to Darcy. For a moment both of them were in the light from the door. And that was when the spell broke and things began to happen swiftly and violently.

A gun boomed from the darkness near the house. Darcy heard the bullet strike home in Jack's plump flesh. Jack gave a choking cry, spun round like a top and crashed backwards into Darcy, deflecting his aim.

Behind them the girl screamed. She came rushing forward. She took one look at Jack's ghastly face and she kept on running.

Darcy had never seen such panic in his life. First Jack, now the girl. He heard Jack sigh, the life bubble from his throat. He let Jack go. There was nothing he could do for him now.

The shot had come from over by the corner of the house somewhere. The small clump of trees maybe.

The girl was still running. Her progress was erratic but it almost seemed as if she was running towards that clump of trees. She was in a state of blind panic and didn't rightly know what she was doing. She was bang in the line of fire.

* * *

Cherokee Pete had acted precipitately. He had seen what he thought was a golden opportunity to get both Fancy Jack and Darcy Kane as they were limmed in the glow of the stable door.

He had been surprised when he saw Kane and he hadn't stopped to think much, hadn't hesitated. He had lugged out his gun and started blasting.

He had had to get Jack first because Jack was in front. He had got Jack, but Jack had fallen against the other man and made things even more difficult. And then when Pete was about to try another shot the girl ran out like a mad Indian and right into the line of fire.

Pete almost shot her. He didn't want to shoot her. He found himself trembling.

He stepped a little way out of cover

and shouted hoarsely, 'Over here, Carmen. Over here!'

Whether she heard him or not, he didn't know. She seemed to be coming right in this direction anyway. He knew she must be in Darcy Kane's line of fire too. He could only hope that Kane wouldn't drop her.

Darcy lost sight of both of them. It was no use shooting blindly into the trees or he might hit the girl. He left Fancy Jack where he lay, his dead eyes staring up at the light. He ran after the bushwhacker and the girl. The kitchen door opened and Big Matt yelled 'Darcy, you all right, Darcy?'

The tall gambler turned in his stride.

Matt came out through the door, a shotgun in his hand.

Darcy said: 'Somebody shot Fancy Jack from cover over here. The girl's loose too.'

'I'll come with you,' said Matt.

Darcy didn't have time to argue with him.

10

A Change of Partner

The girl screamed when the man caught her by the arm, stopping her flight so abruptly that she almost went over backwards.

'It's me, Carmen. Pete!'

She recognized the dark face, the liquid eyes. 'Pete! Did you shoot Jack?'

'I was aiming at Kane,' he said. 'Jack got in the way.' He pulled her. 'Come on, we gotta get away from here. And fast.'

She didn't need any persuading. All she wanted to do was keep on running. They ran together.

Luck was with them.

And besides this Cherokee Pete had a sort of an instinct for the dark ways, the short cuts. He dragged the gasping Carmen with him through fetid alleys, past ashcans and over rubbish dumps, through broken-down picket-fences and past the back doors of tiny cribs and dives.

They reached the back entrance of the grogshop where the rest of the boys waited and he dragged her through after him.

★　★　★

Darcy Kane and Big Matt had lost their quarry completely.

'Looks like the girl went right along with the killer,' said Darcy. 'I guess it was one of those four hardcases. Maybe he wasn't even shooting at Jack but at me and Jack got in the way. Or maybe he wanted to get me too and the girl got in the way. She certainly messed things up.'

The tall gambler swore savagely. 'We all messed thing's up.'

'We better give up for now,' said Matt, 'an' get back to the house. I guess all hell's popping there by now.'

The two men turned around.

Matt said: 'It won't be wise for you to be seen, Darcy. Particularly now there's been another killing and you're in the thick of it . . .

'I'll find another place, Matt. I . . . '

'Let me finish, you pesky son-of-a-gun. I was gonna suggest you slip in the side entrance and go right on up the stairs. Everybody'll be round back and with luck nobody'll spot you. Even if anybody sees you they may not know you or recognize you. The place was bursting. It'll be bursting even more as the night goes on, particularly now we've had a killing. What do you say?'

'You're the boss.'

'All right. You know that little room at the end of the hall, the one you like, the one you've used before when you've visited us? You said it was the quietest room in the house . . . '

'Yeh, I know the one you mean.'

'It's empty. Nobody's got it. Go there. Take yourself a rest an' forget all this for a bit. Here's the key.'

Darcy took the key, said, 'Thanks, old friend.'

Matt peered into the younger man's face as they walked along side by side.

Matt said: 'You had no sleep last night. You wouldn't listen to me an' get your head down during the day. You look pretty awful. You can't find anybody, chase anybody if you're dead on your feet. That makes sense don't it?'

'Yeh, I guess so.'

'You'll do as I say then?'

'Sure, Matt. Thanks for everything.'

'Hell, will yuh shut your silly face!' said Matt, his Texas drawl more scathingly evident than ever.

Darcy grinned tiredly and shut up.

Matt was right all along, of course. Darcy not only looked awful, he felt awful.

They were nearing the house now and could hear the din out back.

Matt said quickly, 'I'll say I heard the shot an' ran out. I didn't see anything, anybody.'

93

'People will remember Jack's girl, they'll have seen her go outside with you . . . '

'They don't remember anything. Not them! Don't worry, Darcy. I'll handle things. Folks know me. I'm proud to say most of 'em trust me.'

'All right, Matt.'

In the trees they separated. Matt went on to the back of the house. Darcy heard him being greeted by the crowd out there. Questions were thrown at him. He heard Matt say: 'I didn't even see him. He got clean away.'

There was nobody near the side door. Darcy went through it. The big room was almost empty. People were clustered at the door that led into the kitchen. Darcy could hear Sadie's voice. He turned right and went up the stairs.

With the key Matt had given him he let himself into the little room at the end of the passage. He lit the lamp. The room, as always, was clean and bright. The colourful Navajo blanket was still on the bed as he remembered it.

He took off his boots, his coat. He undid his shirt. As an afterthought he went back to the door and locked it on the inside. He put his gun beneath the pillow. Then partially-dressed as he was he got underneath the top blanket.

Sleep closed over him like the black waters of a huge lake.

★　★　★

'We've got to get out of here now I guess,' said Greg Burnette. 'The law knows Fancy Jack left the boat with us. They'll be looking for us eventually if only to tell us our friend's been killed.'

'How about the girl?' said squint-eyed Bat McGee. 'They'll be looking for her too. She was with Fancy Jack just before he was killed, Pete says.' He jerked a thumb in the direction of Carmen. 'What shall we do with her?'

Cherokee Pete still had his hand on the girl's arm but in a gentler way now. He said:

'The girl comes with me.'

'Hell,' burst out rat-faced little Sam Konacky. 'I wanted to leave this place all along but I didn't bargain for taking no girl with me.'

'I'll be responsible for her,' said Cherokee Pete in a flat deadly voice.

Sam Konacky looked at the handsome man uncertainly. He opened his mouth as if to say something else but Greg Burnette beat him to it.

'I think that'll be the best. Bring the girl along.'

For once Burnette was being diplomatic.

Carmen did not say anything. She didn't seem to object to coming along with the handsome Cherokee Pete for her protector. Maybe she figured that Pete was an improvement on that little worm, Fancy Jack. Maybe she hadn't realized, beautiful but dumb as she was, that Pete was far deadlier than Jack could ever have been and would toss her away like a spent match when he was finished with her, might even snuff her out completely.

If Darcy Kane caught up with the boys they would have to keep Carmen's mouth shut. And they knew now that Kane had the tenacity of a hungry wolf, he wouldn't give up easily.

11

Men on the Run

The days passed.

Darcy Kane had finally picked up the trail of the four men. He had good reason to believe they had the girl with them.

Probably she had gone of her own free will now that her erstwhile meal-ticket, Fancy Jack, was far out of reach in the land of the lost.

Maybe she had gone with the handsome dark member of the gang. The one who looked like a 'breed. The one they called Cherokee Pete. She had had her eye on him, Darcy knew. Maybe *he* was more of her type than Jack had been. He was probably just as well heeled too.

Darcy knew the law was looking for him. He figured he had shaken them off. Murder or no murder, they were not likely to follow him over the border and into the Western badlands.

But he didn't intend to stay in the West all his life, on the run like so many others. The South was his home, the river, the river towns. He meant to return to them. He meant to clear his name.

If he could take the woman back, he thought she might be induced to help. Particularly if she had found out more about the dead man's companions. Darcy had a feeling about them. He'd had a feeling about them all along, back there on the riverboat even before he killed one of their number.

They were no more 'cattle-buyers' than he was. They were Western hardcases, outlaws most probably. Before he left St Louis he heard the news from Big Matt about the bank-robbery at a town further up the river. It had been pulled by five men and a clerk had been killed. The men had ridden away unscathed.

If Darcy's memory served him rightly, the five men led by the big one in the ten-gallon hat had hopped the river boat not far downriver from the scene of the crime.

Probably they had stashed their horses somewhere, figuring nobody would think of looking for them on a riverboat. They had been right too.

Darcy wished he could get one of them at the point of a gun, make him talk. Or get the girl alone. He had charm just as much as that half-breed or whoever else among the gang that she had tagged along with. Carmen had given him the high sign more than once back on the boat, though, not wishing to mix pleasure with business, he had ignored it.

He was beginning to wish now that he had been nicer to her back there on the boat. If he had, maybe she would have told the truth about the shooting in the first place and he wouldn't be on the run now, wouldn't be both hunter and hunted.

Never trust a woman, he thought.

He was reminded of the golden-haired girl back at the farm by the river. She had been a spirited filly, despite the conditions under which she lived — or maybe because of them. She had tried to rob him, she might even have shot him if he had gotten awkward with her.

But strangely enough, he didn't hold this against her. She had been like a tiger fighting for her young. Fighting for those two little kids, her brother and sister, and for her father, that worn-out old cuss. He didn't even know her name but he thought he would like to see her again some time. He had half promised to see her again, to return, bringing the black stallion.

But he rode the black stallion now. He had not had time to get another horse, and he probably wouldn't have been able to get a faster one anyway. So he had added the stigma of 'horse-thief' to his roster of crimes and this worried him more than the killing did.

The horse hadn't belonged to the girl

and her father. He hoped they weren't in trouble because of its loss. He would have to try and put it right somehow, some day.

He rode; he kept looking, kept asking. His quarry were not actually gamblers like himself, not professionals. But they were gambling men and he knew their sort. If they entered a place where any kind of games were under way they were drawn to the tables like moths to a flame.

On the boat they had all been well-heeled. If Darcy's surmize was correct and they were the bank robbers who were wanted in the South, they were even richer in pocket than he had first assumed.

Darcy knew enough outlaws to realize that their type seldom saved money. They never got money honestly. And once they'd got it they seemed to have a driving compulsion to spend it as quickly as possible in riotous living. Then they went out again and cheated and stole and killed to get some more money. Most of them finished up riddled with bullets from lawmen or from their own kind, or ended their days kicking on the end of a rope.

But Darcy didn't want his men to lie in a gutter or kick on the end of a rope. Not till he'd got to them first any way, made them talk, saved the girl.

Yes, although he was no knight errant, he figured that eventually he'd have to save the girl. If it wasn't too late already.

The first big town he encountered on his travels in the West was Kansas City.

He had had word at various stops he had taken on the road that the four men and the girl were ahead of him. So they were still keeping together it seemed. It also seemed that they were heading for Kansas City. Maybe they planned to light there. He hoped to catch up with them there.

★　★　★

What Darcy Kane did not know was that the boys had planned to split up in Kansas City and go their different ways in ones and twos. And then to meet there again in a month's time to get set for the next job, which Simmons would have gotten figured out in the interim.

But Simmons was dead now and although there were still five of them, the fifth wasn't strictly a member of the gang.

They weren't quite sure what to do, whether to carry on with the original plan or not.

Bat McGee and Sam Konacky always stuck together. The other two were loners. In any case, Cherokee Pete would now take the girl with him.

They gathered in a private room behind a saloon in Kansas City.

Greg Burnette didn't like the girl getting to know too much about their plans so Cherokee Pete took her out front for a while. He said they could do what the hell they liked, he knew what *he* was going to do.

After the door had closed behind Pete and the girl, Bat McGee said:

'I don't like to think of them two goin' off on their own. You know how Pete is about his women. When he gets tired of her, he'll throw her over. She knows too much already. She's liable to blab . . . '

'You're too cautious,' said Greg Burnette. 'She can blab all she likes an' nobody'll take much notice. Time passes. People forget. We're all going further West. Nobody's gonna chase us up here.'

'I don't really like it any more than Bat does,' said Sam Konacky, Bat's pard. 'To tell the truth I think it'd be better for us all to stay together a mite longer. Pete an' the girl too.'

'If Pete will agree to that,' said McGee.

'What do you think, Greg?' asked Konacky.

For once Burnette agreed. 'I think Pete will come round to our way of thinking if we put it to him fair,' he said grimly.

But Cherokee Pete was a moody sort of a cuss. He had taken orders from Simmons all right. But whether he would pay the same heed to Burnette now a decision had to be made was another thing.

Burnette said: 'Anyway, nobody's trying to steal his woman, he can be sure of that. I, for one, don't want Fancy Jack's ex-mistress.'

'You ain't had the chance,' said McGee.

Then he dried up as Burnette gave him a murderous glare. The sandy-haired killer fancied himself with the women. The other two couldn't help wondering whether Burnette wasn't jealous of Cherokee Pete having Carmen, of Cherokee having killed Jack to get her. It was the kind of stunt that Burnette might have pulled himself had he had the chance.

There was no love lost between Burnette and Cherokee Pete, never had been. They were too much alike.

Burnette was indubitably the brainier of the two. He was fastest with a gun too. But Pete was a wizard with a knife, could draw and throw a knife faster than a good many men could pull a gun.

He was a cruel one, too — as cruel as any savage Cherokee — as his new woman would doubtless discover before she was much older.

'Go down and get yourself a drink, Bat,' said Burnette. 'Stay there and watch the girl. Ask Pete if he'll come up and talk to me and Sam.'

With a disgruntled expression on his face the squint-eyed man rose. He didn't say anything but stamped from the room.

After the door had closed behind him, his pard Konacky said: 'Carmen ain't likely to run off with Bat. So Pete needn't be afraid of that.'

Burnette laughed but there was no merriment behind it. He was not a humorous man.

He was keyed up too, waiting for Cherokee Pete, ready to kill him if need be, though that was something he didn't want to pull yet if he could avoid it.

12

The Cut of the Deck

Bat McGee was disgruntled, and he wasn't quite sure why.

He sought out Pete and Carmen who were having a drink at the bar. He nudged the dark man.

'Greg wants to see you.'

Pete turned and scowled at him.

'Whyn't Greg come down here then?'

McGee nudged him again, indicated the girl with a nod of his head. He wasn't over-bright, but he was trying to be circumspect.

'Greg an' Sam want to talk to you about somethin'. I'll stay down here.'

Pete looked at him suspiciously. Then he looked at the girl. He shrugged his broad shoulders. He said: 'I'm going out back for a bit, honey. Stay here will you? Bat'll make sure nobody bothers you.'

Carmen nodded brightly, didn't say anything. Her recent adventures and her change of man seemed to have gone to her head. In many ways Cherokee Pete was better than Fancy Jack had been. But something about Pete scared her as Jack had never done.

Also she was beginning to realize from scraps of conversation she had heard that these men weren't at all what they pretended to be back on the riverboat. They certainly weren't cattle-buyers. Pete had shown no more compunction about killing Fancy Jack than he would have done about destroying a sick dog. And Carmen had an idea that he would have shot Darcy Kane too if she hadn't got in the way.

She was all mixed-up in her mind. Sometimes she wished she had told the truth about Kane and the shooting back on the boat instead of siding with Fancy Jack and these men.

The killing had been pure self-defence on the tall gambler's part. Except for the players she had been nearer to the table than anybody else. She had seen it all.

On the other hand she told herself that she was better off now, that she and Cherokee Pete would do great things together. He was all man. He had plenty of money and he was generous with it. And when that was gone he was the sort who would soon get more. He was nerveless and ruthless.

Deep in her hard mercenary soul, however, Carmen had been fond of Fancy Jack, fonder of him than of any other man she had been with. And there had been plenty of them right from the time she was fourteen and her worthless mother died and she took over her mother's position in a dive in the French quarters of New Orleans.

Jack had been gentler with her than any other man she had met. His fast talking, his cheating and lying, his fancy clothes: they all hid the trembling soul of a coward. He had clung to Carmen, depended on her. He had given her everything that had been in his power to give. And she had comforted him, bolstered his confidence, allowed him to show her off, preen himself beside her.

She had sided with him automatically on the boat although at the time she had thought he was wrong to take the line he did, siding with the four Westerners rather than with a Southerner like himself and a river man into the bargain. She realized now that had Jack taken the straight course at the time instead of the crooked one he might still be alive: surely Cap'n Brunello and his crew could have protected him (and her) from these four hardcases.

But Carmen's life had schooled her to make the best of things, taught her that in the last analysis she must look after herself and say to hell with everybody else. To look after her man too, if she wanted him to look after her.

Cherokee Pete was her man now. He was entirely different to Fancy Jack but even so she thought she knew how to handle him. She'd know better if his three friends weren't at their elbows. And particularly that Greg Burnette! She hated him. He'd kill you without batting an eyelash and get pleasure out of it too. Back in New Orleans she'd met cold-eyed duellists who were the same kind of killers as Greg Burnette. They had made her flesh crawl. Burnette had the same effect on her.

She sensed the friction between Burnette and her own man. She sensed the uncertainty among the four of them and realized that the man with the ten-gallon hat whom Darcy Kane had killed had been their leader and they were still a bit lost without him.

She knew that Greg Burnette wanted to be leader and because he was cleverer than Cherokee Pete he was the one that Bat McGee and Sam Konacky would back if things came to a head.

They were scared of him too. But Pete wasn't scared of him, didn't intend to be pushed in any way by him.

So Carmen was uncertain, as all of them were uncertain. But she was more uncertain than they because she was a woman and at their mercy, particularly if things went wrong with Pete. And she was more uncertain because she was slowly finding out things that they already knew, and these things frightened her.

So she drank and clung to Cherokee Pete, and drank some more.

She didn't really want Pete to leave her there in the bar-room. But she figured she'd be safe. Nobody could harm her among all these people. And Bat McGee was staying behind with her. She didn't like the squint-eyed man, but she didn't fear him the way she feared Greg Burnette.

She wasn't sure whether McGee was there to protect her — hell, she didn't need protection: she had been raised in places like this! — or whether he was there to make sure she didn't get away.

But where would she go if she got away? She'd be better off if she played out her hand, tried to get Pete loose from the rest. She could handle him then: she had handled dangerous men before.

Anyway, she was a bit too drunk to worry unnecessarily at the moment.

★   ★   ★

Bat McGee stood by the girl and took a drink of rye and continued to be disgruntled.

'How's Bat?' asked Carmen in a little-girl sort of voice.

He looked at her. Hell, she was getting drunk. That was all they needed now, a drunken dame.

'Bat's all right,' he said harshly.

She pouted. She's a mighty fine looking woman, thought McGee. But she was Cherokee Pete's woman and he didn't want any trouble with Pete. Right now he didn't want any trouble with anybody. He didn't rightly know what he did want. He wasn't even sure whether it was best for them all to stay together a while longer instead of him and Sam going off together as in the past, meeting up with the others weeks later.

He couldn't help feeling that had Cherokee Pete plugged this girl when he plugged her man things would be a whole lot simpler. All they'd have to worry about then was the law and maybe that gambler, Darcy Kane, if he was still on the loose.

The law had never bothered them much before. They knew more holes to hide in than a bunch of gophers. McGee took another sidelong look at the girl. He took another drink too and he stood and brooded, his cross-eyes staring at nothing.

Recognizing his mood and the fact that he didn't want to talk, the girl was silent too. She could have been brooding too.

McGee leaned his elbow on the bar,

one foot on the brass rail and turned to survey the room. He noticed that a few folks — men mainly — were watching him and the dark girl. That was understandable. She was easily the best looking filly in the room.

She's with me now, McGee thought, and began to preen himself. Although he didn't realize it, he acted rather the way Fancy Jack used to act when Carmen was with him.

Because of his unprepossessing appearance, his yellow face, his squint eyes, McGee had never had much luck with women. He had never before had anything to do with a young woman as handsome, as shapely, as beautifully-dressed as Carmen. This fact, and the liquor, began to go to his head.

He saw that there was a faro layout nearby. He would have taken notice of this sooner or later, for he was an inveterate gambler and a wild one too: here was where most of his ill-gotten gains usually went.

He pinched the girl and she gave a

little squeak. She turned on him half-angrily, half-coquettishly. She couldn't help being coquettish. It was part of her training, part of her make-up.

McGee said: 'Let me an' you go buck the tiger, honey. You give me luck, huh? Like you useter give Fancy Jack luck.' He guffawed at what he considered to be a good joke.

The girl hesitated for a moment. Then she said, 'All right, let's go.'

13

A Deal in Death

Bat McGee bet heavily. He didn't seem to know any other way to bet.

He lost. Each time he lost he stepped up his bid. And suddenly he began to win. He turned and grinned at the girl, his cross-eyes alight with triumph.

'You with the bat-eyes,' said the dealer silkily. 'Watch your cards.'

The dealer was a sneakish-looking individual with a pencil-thin moustache on a face like a death's head. He couldn't have known that McGee's nickname was Bat but that only Bat's friends were allowed to address him that way.

'Bat-eyes' was a very bad choice of epithet for the dealer to use, particularly while the girl was there to hear it.

The dealer, although his deathly

poker-face did not reveal the fact, was boiling with rage because the cross-eyed man's fortune had changed and he was on a winning streak, winning heavily. The bank just could not stand it.

The dealer made the mistake others had made before him and lived to regret it, if they lived at all. He had taken the cross-eyed man for a simpleton.

Also, as the dealer had a derringer in reach of his hand on the tiny specially-built shelf beneath the table he didn't think he had anything to fear from this cross-eyed gink anyway. He had to stop his winning streak somehow, and that was a fact. Maybe if he got him rattled . . .

He got him rattled all right.

But McGee leaned forward a little, his belly pressed against the edge of the table, his left hand on the top of it, his right hand beneath it. His thin face was yellower than ever. His cross-eyes looked at some point way over the dealer's head.

'Would you like to repeat that, friend?' he said. 'Would you like to repeat what you just said?'

Something about those cross-eyes had subtly changed and the dealer wasn't sure whether he liked this. But he had accomplished what he had set out to do. Accomplished it more quickly even than he had expected. And so went through with it. His fingers crawled towards the derringer on its little shelf beneath the table. He had forgotten what his actual words had been so he intoned:

'I said pick up your cards, bat-eyes.'

And he went for the derringer.

The top half of the other man's body did not move. But the yellow face worked a little and the cross-eyes flared as he shot the dealer from under the table. He shot him twice in the belly so that he was crashed backwards by the force of the heavy slugs.

He finished half across another table, scattering the people who had been seated around it, crying out, a woman screaming. When the table stopped rocking, he was spread-eagled across it, flat on his back, crucified beneath the bright lights.

He had cried out at first. He had kicked a little.

But now he was quite dead, the sudden silence in the big packed room was like a warm, clogging blanket. Then two men moved up behind Bat McGee and stuck guns in his ribs and one of them said, 'We're deputies, mister, we'll take that.' And reached over Bat's shoulder and snatched the still-smoking Colt from his hand.

'The woman,' said somebody. 'Stop the woman!'

★ ★ ★

Carmen was running again, just the way she had run when Fancy Jack had been killed. In cases like this she took the line of least resistance. Her instinct was to run like hell. So she ran.

Instinctively too, however, she ran in

the right direction. Not towards the street, for there would be no escape there, but towards the back room where Cherokee Pete and the other two sat.

Startled by the shot, they were already on their feet and Pete, who had been nearest to the door, was halfway towards it when she burst in.

From behind Pete, Greg Burnette drew his gun. Carmen didn't think she had ever seen anybody so fast, except perhaps Darcy Kane.

'You almost got yourself shot, girl,' said the hatchet-faced man thinly. 'What's going on? What was that shot?'

'McGee killed a dealer,' Carmen gasped. 'He had to. But they've got him now.'

Cherokee Pete had already passed through the door.

'Stay here,' snapped Burnette to the girl.

Then he and Sam Konacky followed Pete.

The girl hesitated by the table. Her

dark eyes were scared, full of a horrible uncertainty.

She looked about her. Her cloak was draped over a chair where she had left it. Like a walking doll she went over to it, put it on, fastened it at the throat.

There was another door at the opposite end to the room from the one through which she had entered. It was locked but the key was on the inside. She turned the key, let herself out.

She found herself in a passage dimly-lit by a hanging hurricane-lamp with the wick turned down. There was a curtain at one end, a narrow door at the other. She made for the door.

This one, too, was locked and again the key was on the inside.

She let herself out into the dark night, the cool damp air behind the saloon.

If she could work her way round to the front now and get a horse! She and the boys had come to Kansas City by stagecoach and she wasn't dressed for riding, didn't have any riding togs in fact. But she figured she'd manage, she'd have to.

There had been another killing. These men thought nothing of killing. The future was uncertain for her this way. She meant to try and get back across the border, back to St Louis maybe.

14

The Way the Cards Fall

Bat McGee was still trapped in the centre of the saloon near to the faro table, the dead man.

The two deputies still had their guns on him. Other folks were clustered around, pressing in tighter, all yelling at once. Some were for the stranger, saying that it had been self-defence. Others were against him. The dead dealer seemed to have quite a percentage of hardcase friends rooting for him.

There was the usual lunatic element that sensed sport and were calling for a hang-rope, a quick lynch-party to even things up, two dead men instead of just one. Because these, backed by the ex-dealer's friends, were the most vocal and the most violent they were getting the upper hand and the deputies and their captive were becoming hard-pressed.

Hands plucked at Bat McGee's clothes, fists were shaken in his face. A sly blow to his kidneys made him bend over, gasping with pain.

'Give me a gun, goddamn it,' he said.

'Sorry, friend,' said one of the deputies, the one who seemed to be handling himself the best. He turned on the mob. 'I don't want to hafta shoot any of you.'

'You wouldn't do that, Fred,' yelled a voice from the crowd.

'He can't shoot us all,' jeered another one. 'Rush him.'

This voice came from the back of the crowd, as this sort of voice always did.

Fred's pardner looked scared. 'What we gonna do, Fred?' he said in an undertone.

'We're gonna get through,' said Fred, who was a big purposeful-looking youngster. 'Come on.' He began to break a way through the crowd, waving his gun.

★   ★   ★

Three other men, not part of the crowd, had been doing some moving around too.

Cherokee Pete had made his way easily and unnoticed around the edge of the crowd and now stood in front of the batwings.

Greg Burnette and Sam Konacky had remained at the other end of the room but they had separated, spread out.

The three of them now formed a triangle with Cherokee Pete as their apex. And the deputies, with Bat McGee in tow, were breaking their way through to the batwings and to Pete.

He waited till they were almost in the open, although the pack was still baying at their heels, then he raised his hand as a signal to his two pardners.

Burnette and Konacky drew their

guns and Burnette shouted:

'Everybody stay still and don't nobody make any false moves or we'll start shooting.'

There was dead silence. Into this Cherokee Pete threw his two-cents worth from the door.

'That means you,' he said and his gun menaced the deputies.

Fred made the mistake of raising his weapon and Pete shot him in the shoulder. Fred's Colt fell to the boards as the young man staggered and collapsed. Bat McGee bent, grabbed the gun, turned it on Fred's pard. But this worthy had already dropped his own gun in sheer terror.

McGee grabbed this too and backed until he had joined Pete at the batwings.

Now Burnette yelled. 'We want everybodies' paws in the air. Pronto. Or we'll start shooting and we ain't particular who we hit.'

A forest of hands went up.

'Over against the wall everybody,'

yelled Burnette. His pale eyes had a glitter. He was enjoying himself. He looked quite capable of commencing blasting just for the hell of it.

'*Over there! Move!*'

The crowd began to move over to the wall.

The space in front of the bar became clear except for the body of the dealer and Fred and the deputy. Fred began to climb slowly to his feet now, clutching his wounded shoulder, blood dripping through his fingers.

There were two barmen and one of them thought he saw his opportunity. He lugged a shotgun from beneath the bar.

Greg Burnette had been waiting for somebody to make a move like this. He shot the barman in the head. The man crashed backwards into a row of bottles. Glass splintered and the smell of raw hooch filled the air.

The second barman stood white-faced, as if petrified. As far as he was concerned the shotgun could now lie where it was until Kingdom Come, lie there beside his friend's dead body. Brick always had been a reckless cuss . . .

The ranks of people stood against the wall with their hands held aloft. They might have been waiting for a firing squad. The wounded deputy joined them. He was allowed to lean against the wall.

'There's a man here bleedin' to death,' said somebody in a tight savage voice.

'There'll be more if you don't stay still,' said Greg Burnette.

Nobody else said anything. They had been shocked to silence by the swift death of the barman. And the hatchet-faced man with the sandy hair looked as if he enjoyed killing, as if all he needed was another excuse.

Followed by Sam Konacky, Burnette began to move over to the batwings.

The four of them, the two by the batwings and the two moving ones, kept their guns levelled at the folks all the while. It was evident this wasn't the first time they had pulled this kind of stunt.

Konacky said softly to Burnette: 'How about the girl?'

'Get her!'

Konacky retraced his steps. But he soon returned.

'She's gone,' he growled. 'Her cloak's gone. I figure she must've got scared an' slipped out the back way.'

'So she's gone,' said Burnette. 'So to hell with her.' He called over to the door. 'Bat, watch the street.'

The squint-eyed McGee nodded and slipped out through the batwings.

Burnette said to Konacky, 'We might as well make the most of this while we're about it. Strip the bar an' the gaming tables, grab all the money you can find.'

Konacky holstered his gun, moved, worked fast. When they had been short of a buck they had more than once stuck bar-rooms up. Sometimes the haul had been quite rich. He took off his neckcloth and made it into a pouch.

When he had made his rounds this pouch sagged heavily with money.

'Let's go,' said Burnette.

They moved over to the batwings.

There were people in the dark street. They were staring, coming slowly nearer. But, as yet, Bat McGee hadn't had to shoot anybody. Speculation was rife about the shooting. But although people were curious, they didn't intend to stick their necks out.

Burnette said: 'Grab four horses. It's time we had some.'

'Where's Carmen?' said Cherokee Pete.

'We don't know. She ran out the back way.'

Pete looked as if he was about to go back through the bar-room and look for her.

Burnette said quickly: 'You'll have to leave her, Pete. She'll come to no harm. She can catch up with us later if she wants to.'

Pete saw the sense of this.

Burnette backed out last. All he

wanted was somebody else to make a fool move, that was all. That was all he wanted . . .

★   ★   ★

Carmen had taken a horse without being spotted. She was riding hard, her skirts hitched back over her silk-clad knees. Her legs, long though they were, only just managed to reach the stirrups. She hadn't had time to fix the saddle or anything properly and she didn't intend to stop and try until she'd put plenty of space between herself and Kansas City.

She rode hard. She drove the horse, which was a spavined nag and needed driving. It was the first horse she had spotted at the hitching-rail outside the saloon. Goaded by her own panic she hadn't had time to make a selection and she was no judge of horseflesh anyway.

She didn't like horses and never rode one if she could possibly avoid it. She didn't like the dark night and the open countryside either. She had been brought up among the bright lights. They were her natural element. These and people and noise and colour and fun and men.

And now she was alone. No man to protect her. No lights. Just the wide dirt road leading out of Kansas City and miles of rolling open land each side of her. She hoped she wouldn't run into any desperate characters. She didn't even have a gun. She was almost penniless also. All she had were her fancy clothes, as inappropriate to a horse-ride in the countryside, by dark or by day, as an Easter bonnet on a bull.

There was a pale moon now but this was little help to her peace of mind. It gave everything an eerie look. Trees beside the road looked like tall men waiting to pounce and the smaller vegetation and outcrops of rock crouched like menacing beasts.

She did not hear the horseman approaching from the other direction.

135

He had heard her first. He had stopped and drawn his mount into the shadows.

Then, when she drew abreast, he kneed the horse forward.

The girl gasped. The moonlight fell on the man's face and, although she could hardly believe her eyes, she didn't think she had ever been so glad to see anybody in her life before.

She spoke his name like a cry.

'*Darcy Kane!*'

15

Plans

'You've certainly messed things up now,' said Burnette to Bat McGee.

The cross-eyed man was sullen and peevish. He said: 'That dealer threw down on me. What did you want me to do, just stand there an' let myself get plugged? What would you have done?'

There was no answer needed for this, not even from Burnette himself. Everybody knew what Greg Burnette would have done.

'I wonder what happened to the girl,' said Cherokee Pete.

'I don't figure we'll see her again,' said Burnette. 'It doesn't matter now anyway. She can talk her head off if she wants to. After what happened in Kansas City we'll have the law after us here too.'

'That's gonna confuse 'em,' chuckled Sam Konacky. 'We can forget about the Southern job I guess. We're plenty well-heeled now anyway. On top of the bank money we've got the stuff I picked up in the saloon. That wasn't a bad haul y'know.'

'Let's dib it up then,' said Bat McGee.

The four men were crouched in an abandoned cabin they had found. There was no furniture, just old boxes. These served as seats, however, and a larger packing case was the table. On top of this light flickered from a stub of candle that somebody had found.

Sam Konacky undid the pouch he had made from his large kerchief. He tipped the contents on top of the pack case. Crumpled rolls of bills in various stages, some worn, dirty, all legal tender. Coins of the larger denomination. A couple of small bags of gold dust. A few fairly valuable pieces of jewellery which had been taken in payment of debts.

Burnette poked among the stuff. 'What's this?' he said. It was a ring with a large stone set in the centre. Cherokee Pete picked it up. He had the keenest eyes among them. He held it close to the flame of the candle and got his head down there and scrutinized the ring.

'Is it a diamond, Pete?' said Sam Konacky.

'It might well be. Can't tell for sure though, particularly in this light.'

'There is one place we'd be able to find out,' said Burnette. 'An' I was thinking of making for there anyway.'

'Hangtown?' said Bat McGee.

Burnette nodded. 'That's it. We've thrown that posse off the trail for a bit I guess. But we're not out of the woods yet. If we can get to Hangtown we can hole up there for a bit. If we're traced to there by a big number of lawmen we'll find out about it soon enough.'

He looked about him at the lowering faces in the flickering candlelight.

'We stick together you mean?' said Cherokee Pete.

'Why not?'

'Yeh, I suppose you're right.' Pete was still turning the ring slowly around between his thumb and finger. It winked dully as it caught the pale light.

Bat McGee and his pard Konacky had exchanged glances.

McGee said, 'It's all right by me an' Sam.'

'God, I'm hungry,' said Konacky. 'I wish I'd taken some food and a couple of bottles of liquor while I was stripping that saloon.'

'We'll get food as soon as we can,' said Greg Burnette. 'There's none in this rat-trap, that's certain sure. It's time we got moving I guess.'

He rose. Sam Konacky put the money and jewellery back where it came from. Rather reluctantly it seemed, Cherokee Pete gave him the ring.

'It's a helluva way from here to Hangtown,' said Bat McGee.

'Then the sooner we get started the better,' said Burnette.

Hangtown was one of the most notorious hell-holes of the West. There were many hell-holes in these lawless times. But most of them had a semblance of law, a killer marshal, a vigilante committee, a mayor and town council, a sheriff or a couple of deputies. But Hangtown had no law at all except that of King Colt.

It was a rendezvous for outlaws, a hideout for men on the run. Its population fluctuated constantly and was never very large. But it was always wild and always cosmopolitan. The strangest people turned up in Hangtown. Some of them stayed. The town had a nucleus of regular citizens all of whom were either quick with wits or gun or with both, or in a few cases, were so insignificant that nobody looked for them any more anyway.

A lawman alone or with only a few friends took his life and the lives of others in his hands if he entered Hangtown on business. Occasionally a posse of some strength raided the town.

Sometimes they got who they were after, sometimes they didn't.

There had been talk about sending the military in, driving everybody out, burning this pestilent spot to the ground. But some of its top citizens, on the fringes of lawlessness though they were, had riches and powerful friends. And nothing was done.

Hangtown sweltered and spawned and screamed in its hollow in the arid lands. No good people would live there it was said, no parents would want to raise a family there: there was no land, no sustenance, water had to be transported from the river miles away and peddled by the cask. But there were families there, of a kind, families who preyed on hard-pressed visitors and got fat on misery and human degradation.

All the vices of Creation, the large ones, the small ones, the vile ones, the petty ones: they were all gathered in this hell-hole sunk in the dry Western plains.

A man could have freedom there, of a

sort. Freedom from the law perhaps. But he paid for that freedom in other ways.

But the quartet of killers who planned to visit Hangtown now knew the place of old and didn't intend to pay for anything if they could possibly help it.

16

On the Scent

Darcy Kane didn't intend to waste too much time on the girl, Carmen.

He owed her nothing. Far from it. Had she played straight back there on the riverboat he would not be where he was now. And *what* he was: both hunted and hunter.

But she was willing to talk now. She admitted her mistake, said she would like to put it right as soon as she could. She also told him things about the four so-called cattle-buyers that made him sure that what he had suspected about them was true. They, with their friend in the ten-gallon hat, were the gang who had robbed the Southern bank and killed a young teller.

Carmen told Darcy how she had run away after the killing in the saloon in

Kansas City. Darcy's first instinct was to go on right away, leave her there in the road. But she was in great distress and was vindicating herself as fast as she could. And, anyway, he'd always had a soft spot for the ladies. So he retraced his steps, rode back with her to the next small town which had a stage coach halt.

He paid for her seat for the following morning and gave her some more money to be going on with. She would he able to make her way to St Louis as she had planned. A hostler promised to return the horse she had taken back to Kansas City. Darcy wouldn't have trusted the man any further than he could have thrown him with one arm. But Darcy himself had one stolen horse on his hands already and that was enough for him.

'Why not come back with me to St. Louis, Darcy?' Carmen pleaded. 'I can clear your name now. You don't have to go after those men. They're killers and you're on your own. Let the law handle it. I'll tell them all I know. I'll tell them anything. Please come back with me, Darcy.'

'I can't, Carmen, don't you see? I've come this far and I can't turn back, particularly now I've found out what I discovered about them is true. They started this thing. I've got to finish it if I can . . .'

'It's pride,' burst out the girl. 'Just pride. Silly men's pride.'

'You may be right, honey. But I can't turn back now . . .'

'I'll come back with you to Kansas City then. I'll talk to the law there.'

'No, Carmen. It's too risky. You're a danger to those men don't you see? They'll get you if they can . . . Besides, you'll slow me up. Tomorrow you go on to St Louis, y'understand?'

'All right, Darcy,' said the girl wearily, 'I'll do what you say.'

'Go to Big Matt and tell him all you've told me. He'll know what to do. He'll pass it on to the proper authorities. He'll also clear me, too.'

'I'll be glad to do that anyway,' said Carmen.

There was silence for a bit. Then Darcy said slowly: 'I'm sorry about Fancy Jack, Carmen.'

'He wasn't much of a man I guess. But he was good to me.' The girl's voice broke suddenly. 'And I went off with the one who killed him . . . '

'Maybe he meant to kill me really,' said Darcy. 'If that's any consolation.'

'I must've been crazy to go with Cherokee Pete anyway — that killer!'

'Forget it! Put it behind you.'

'I wish things had been different though — different from a long time ago. Come back to St Louis with me, please, Darcy.'

'No, Carmen. I'm sorry. I'm riding on right now, tonight. I'm trusting you to catch that stage tomorrow, to do everything I've asked.'

'I will, Darcy. I promise.'

She reached upwards quickly and put her arms around his neck. She kissed him full on the lips. Her own lips were trembling and hot.

She pulled away from him then. She ran across the lobby of the hotel in which Darcy had got her a room for the night. She fled up the stairs, leaving him standing in the lobby under the curious gaze of the spotty-faced clerk.

Women are funny critturs, thought Darcy. He certainly hadn't expected sentimentality, a sort of tenderness, a sort of shyness even from that filly of all people. He gave the clerk a glare and the youth dropped his gaze.

Darcy strode from the hotel lobby, went right to the hitching rack, unhitched the black stallion, and mounted him.

There was no time to be wasted.

Kansas City next stop.

★　　★　　★

It was late when he got there. He might have expected that most of the town would be sleeping. But instead the place was full of lights and hurrying people.

From a hostler at the livery stables, Darcy learned what had happened. Two men killed and another wounded; a saloon robbed; four men on the run.

A small posse had already lit out after them. Another larger one was now being formed.

The elderly wizened hostler was pretty sardonic about it all. Hadn't been so much hoo-ha since a local banker killed his wife with a hatchet and hung himself from the old peeled cottonwood by the horse-trough in the middle of main street.

'The marshal's outa town,' explained the hostler, 'Gone to a lawmans' conference or sump'n, if there are such things. His best deputy, Fred, got himself shot in the shoulder tryin' to buck them killers. The other deputy ain't much good, though he did take the first posse out — he couldn't do much else I guess.

'Now everybody an' his brother is going with this second bunch. They'll probably finish up by shooting it out with the first posse by mistake or plugging each other in the dark. I figure those four killers were professionals. No wild posse is gonna catch 'em. No two wild posses even, making as much goddamned noise as a wagon-train full of screaming monkeys. Just listen to 'em down there!'

Darcy could hear them. They were making enough noise to wake the two dead men who lay in the town this night.

Most of the so-called posse seemed to be drunk. There was a lot of shouting and the uttering of dire threats; a man waved a coiled rope in the air and, his other hand at his throat, lurched and gurgled in drunken pantomime; another man shot a gun repeatedly in the air until it was empty; two more had flaming torches, though it could not be clear what they intended to do with them.

'All the blood-lusting scum of the town,' said the elderly hostler bitterly. 'The town marshal ain't a bad gink, if a mite old. It's a pity he ain't here. He has the experience, he'd have got things better organized anyway.'

Darcy decided to take this bitter but level-headed elderly man into his confidence. He might be some help now or later, though, right then, Darcy couldn't figure out in what way this might be.

The tall gambler said: 'I came here looking for those four men. They're wanted for a bank robbery down South.'

The man's face took on a guarded look. 'You a lawman?'

'No, just a private citizen at the moment. A gambler by profession. There were five men in that gang to begin with. I killed the fifth one in a gunfight, gave him an even break . . . '

'There was a girl with them when they came to town. Are you after the girl?'

'I've seen the girl. She's on her way back to St Louis now. Back there they don't know yet that those four men are wanted. They're still looking for me for killing the fifth one . . . '

The man's face sharpened. 'And you aim to clear yourself?'

'The girl will do that for me.'

'Still,' said the hostler, 'you're taking a crazy chance going after four hardcases like that on your lonesome.'

'I know that, friend. Now I figure I'm in the clear as far as that killing was concerned I was aiming to consult the law here. Get a bit of official backing, at least. A deputy's badge maybe. When will the town marshal be back?'

'Not till tomorrow I guess.'

'I certainly can't wait that long.'

'Go see Fred the deputy then. He's only got a busted shoulder an' I'm told he's already talking his head off, wants to go after the one who shot him. Regular wild killer that was it seems, one of that gang. Sandy-haired, face like a wolf.'

That would be Greg Burnette, Darcy thought. He knew those four now better than he had ever done. Carmen's story about them had been pretty vivid.

'Where can I find Fred the deputy?'

'I'll take you to him,' said the hostler. He raised his voice. 'Jobey.'

A sleepy-eyed youth slouched from the darkness in back of the stables.

'Keep an eye on things till I get back. If any of that mob bother you get the shotgun out.'

The lad livened up considerably. 'Right,' he said brightly.

'Come on, young feller.'

Darcy left his horse. He followed his guide.

17

On the Trail

Fred the deputy was propped up in bed in a little room beside the local jail. He was arguing with a grizzled little man who proved to be the local doctor. Fred wanted to get up and go out and join Patsy.

Patsy it seemed was the other deputy.

Patsy was so useless, by all accounts, that Darcy could not figure why he had been made deputy in the first place. 'You wouldn't catch up with him now anyway,' said the doctor.

'Hark at that mob outside then. I oughta do something about that.'

'Got a visitor for you, Fred,' said the hostler. The lean young deputy squinted suspiciously at the tall stranger.

'Who are you?'

Darcy told him; told him everything. His story made sense. Fred began to look less suspicious, more interested. Finally, although the little doctor seemed on the point of objection, Fred gave Darcy a deputy's badge.

The gambler dropped it in his pocket, 'I'll only use it if I need to. It'll certainly help me to get information more quickly . . . '

He paused.

Then he went on. 'Here's what I figure I'll do. I don't intend to mix in with a posse, I figure I'll do more good on my own in picking up the gang's trail. And I'll leave a trail behind me, leave word with people here and there so that you or the marshal will be able to follow me.'

'Sounds feasible,' said the young deputy and he started to get out of bed.

The little doctor shoved him in the chest, forced him to recline again. Fred's face went white. A thin film of sweat broke out on his forehead. He evidently wasn't as tough as he thought.

'All right,' he said savagely. 'I'll wait till Ben gets back. But no later.'

The marshal, it seemed, was Ben Galloway. Darcy had heard of him. He'd had quite a rep in the old days. Darcy had thought he was dead. He must be pretty old . . .

'I'll wash up and have a quick bite and a drink an' then I'll be on my way,' he said.

'My boy'll have your hoss ready,' said the little hostler. 'You can do all the rest of it back there too.'

'Thanks, friend.'

'Forget it. Hell, if I was younger an' hadn't got a family to look after, I'd saddle up an' ride with you.'

Darcy shook hands with Fred the deputy.

He received a somewhat grudging handclasp from the little doctor too, who, being a pillar of the community evidently mistrusted gambling killers more than a mite.

'I shan't be far behind you, Mr Kane,' was Fred's parting shot.

He winked at Darcy while the doctor's expression became pained again. Then the tall gambler shut the door behind the hostler and himself. He followed the little elderly man back the way he had come.

★ ★ ★

Although to other people Darcy Kane might have seemed to be bursting with confidence he had never thought his self-imposed task would be easy. He had known he was literally taking his life in his hands. But it was too late to turn back now.

He didn't want to turn back. He had hate for these men. Not only for what they had done to him but for what they had done to others. They were mad dogs who should be put down.

Darcy was no moralist. He lived on the fringes of the law himself. Many of his friends were crooks and ex-owlhooters. These were lawless days. Morals were sketchy and life was cheap.

157

Many a man toting a badge — as Darcy was now — had a few scant years before been chased half-across the West by the very law he now represented.

But towns were eager for tough, fast-shooting sheriffs, deputies and marshals who would help to prevent the wild bunches from taking over completely. If a gunfighter was willing to risk his skin for the comparatively low wages, dignitaries of hardpressed towns did not look too closely into a man's past.

Pardons could be got too, if a man's record wasn't too black; memories were short; many a man who had ridden the owlhoot trail in his youth became in middle-age, whether lawman or not, a respected family-man and pillar of his community.

So Darcy Kane who, within fairly wide limits, had always tried to play things straight, did not feel strange about toting a badge. In any case, he didn't intend to pin it on his breast unless he had to.

It would do to show people, he thought sardonically, help to loosen their tongues. Although, recognising him for what he was, some of them might regard him a little askance.

★ ★ ★

He was able to ride from Kansas City before the second so-called posse started out. He went along the backs of the buildings so that none of them would spot him. He didn't want to be shot at by some drunken hothead who thought any stranger was fair game.

He rode hard the rest of that night and at dawn he almost caught up with the first posse, the one led by the incompetent deputy called Patsy.

But Darcy evaded this bunch too, making a wide swoop, keeping in cover like an Indian scout. He figured that if the posse had lit out right after the four killers they ought, at least, to be on the right trail, and so he was too.

From the cover of a clump of trees

on the brow of a hill he gazed back at the straggling bunch. They looked tired, as if they were ready to give up at any moment.

That was the way with hastily-gathered posses with no proper leader, no proper savvy of what they were out to do.

This bunch had probably started out breathing fire and vengeance and forgotten to bring enough chow and water with them; had forgotten to make sure maybe that their horses had been fed and watered properly too.

A few of them might be getting scared now that the first flash of enthusiasm or bravado had died. They were beginning to wonder what would happen if they did catch up with those desperate killers. Daylight would be here soon and they had been riding hard. They were not gunfighters, hunters; a few of them could be picked off by bushwhackers or snipers before they knew what had hit them.

Darcy wheeled his horse about and

eased him down the other side of the rise. The black stallion responded nobly to everything that was expected of him. They were great friends by now, the magnificent horse and the tall, soft-spoken man with the gentle hands.

It was easy for Darcy to feel that the horse was his own. It seemed so easy, too, for the horse to act as if he had never had any other master.

The flying hooves continued to eat up the miles and the morning broke completely, the sky red like the flush of pounding blood.

Full daylight came and Darcy began to look for signs.

★ ★ ★

In his youth along the Mississippi he had known backwoodsmen and Indian fighters who could read stories in a crushed leaf, a scratched branch, a scuffmark in the dust. The young Darcy had never forgotten the things he had learned. He put them to good use now.

161

Four horsemen made plenty of signs.

They were old hands; they veered off the straight and narrow. He followed their tortuous tracks till they led him to the disused cabin where they had spent part of the night. They would have thrown the posse off with very little difficulty at all.

Darcy was tired. He knew that the bunch wouldn't keep on running indefinitely. They would be bound to light some place. It was only a matter of time.

Maybe Marshal Ben Galloway from Kansas City — not to forget his wounded deputy, Fred — would get to Darcy before he caught his quarry. He'd probably need some help at that. In a stand-up gunfight he might be able to fade any one or two of those killers. But four at once was a different proposition. He didn't aim to commit suicide. The way he saw it, if the marshal and his deputy did not catch up, his best plan would be to try and separate the four men.

As far as he could judge by reading sign they were still together.

Did they aim to stay that way?

His task would be harder if they split and went in opposite ways. If not harder, longer.

He was tired. He wouldn't think. He decided to rest awhile here at this cabin, the way they had rested before him. They had left evidence of themselves behind them among the empty boxes. A few cigarette stubs. A dirty piece of rag that had served as a handkerchief. An empty lucifer-box. Their boots had scuffed the dirt.

If they had stayed here longer and he could have crept up on them what a different morning this would have been!

This cabin had held their evil, their stink. It seemed to linger in the air behind them . . .

But Darcy Kane was not usually given to fancies and he soon pushed this one from his mind. He unsaddled the horse and tethered him to a stump outside. He knew the beast would warn him if anybody approached. He swept a stub of candle from the top of an empty packing-case and he laid himself down there.

In a short while he slept.

18

The Animal and the Free

When he awoke the hut was unpleasantly warm with the growing sun that had beat down on it from outside.

He took his heavy hunter watch from his vest-pocket, extracted it from its skin pouch. He had been asleep for an hour and a half. It was time he moved again.

The atmosphere of the hut was smelly and stifling. The black stallion heard him moving about and whinnied softly.

'I'm coming, boy,' he said.

He stretched his cramped limbs.

The gun he had borrowed from Big Matt was a long-barrelled Colt. It was too big to fit in Darcy's shoulder-holster so he had tucked it into his belt. Its position there was uncomfortable however. As he lay sleeping the gun had dug into his groin and he felt as if somebody had given him a low body blow.

He opened the door of the hut and looked out. The morning was peaceful and hot. The stallion put his head on one side and cocked an inquiring eye.

He whinnied again as if to say 'What's keeping you, my friend?'

'Be with you in a minute, boy,' said Darcy.

He took off his shoulder-holster.

These were quite a new thing. Although duellists in the South used them more frequently now, Darcy didn't think they were so popular here in the West. Dress was different for one thing and the horse was more used, without the carriage. People didn't dress so well to the West as they did in the South. A man thought more of his weapons and his horse than he did of his clothes.

His gun, his horse: they were essentials, his means for survival.

He carried his hardware where it could be seen; he swaggered with it. If he had an overweening vanity he notched the butt of his gun when he killed a man. He probably thought there was something furtive about a shoulder-holster.

But a gun in a shoulder-holster was as much a means of survival as one low-slung at a hip, tied to the thigh by a whang-string, the trigger filed down, the hammer on a hair-spring. These extra refinements were all calculated to increase the speed of the draw, the fire-power.

But opinion was growing, particularly in the South, that a shoulder-draw was faster than a draw from the waist or low at the hip. The hand didn't have so far to travel to reach the gun and it was already at breast height, the best level from which to cut a man down.

It was also just as effective if a man was in an awkward position, such as sitting down.

Some of these Westerners could fire

like lightning from the hip; they could bring their free hand across and 'fan' the hammer of the gun. But very often from such a lower position you needed more than one shot to hit your man in a vital spot. And he was shooting at you at the same time and was likely to score a lucky bull before you did.

Darcy Kane had spent time in the West before. He remembered a gunfight he had once seen on a dusty trailstreet. The best gun-duel he had ever seen in his life. The two opponents drawing their pistols as they advanced slowly towards each other, then raising the pistols to shoulder height and pointing them with straight arms.

The one who had drawn and shot most hastily had missed his target completely. Then a bullet from his opponent's gun had hit him squarely in the forehead and no further shooting had been needed.

On the other hand, Darcy had witnessed other gun-duels in which men, quick on the draw but not good marksmen, had emptied their weapons at each other and had still both lived, shot to rags maybe, crippled but still living.

No, in grandstand plays on dusty streets where the range was often long it wasn't always the man who was quickest on the draw who always emerged as the final victor.

But at close quarters, in a bar-room perhaps, across a table a quick draw was an asset. It often meant the difference between life and death. As it had done in the case of Darcy and the man in the ten-gallon hat on the riverboat. The latter, a professional gunfighter, had used a low-slung draw. Darcy had used his shoulder-draw.

Darcy had lived. The other man had died.

The tall gambler figured he had to keep to his shoulder-holster.

He opened it a little with his fingers, tore the threads. Finally he was able to fit in the long-barrelled Colt into the holster.

He strapped the harness on again. The gun, pouched there, felt a mite heavier than his old one. But he figured he would soon get accustomed to that.

He tried a few practice draws. They were not at all bad. He was quite dispassionate about these manoeuvres, these rehearsals for slaughter. He was a hunter now. He knew that when he caught up with his quarry he would have less compunction about shooting them down — if they didn't get him first — than he would have about killing a wild animal.

A wild animal when he killed was at least only following his natural instincts.

These men were worse than wild animals. There were too many of them running loose in the West today. A few less might even things up a bit, give the better-type people a chance.

Darcy Kane was a cat who prowled by himself. He had no great fondness for the straightforward 'better-type' life. But at least he only preyed on his own kind.

Grinning sardonically he took his deputy's badge out of his vest-pocket. He rubbed it on his sleeve until it shone. The sunlight caught it and it seemed to come alive and wink at him derisively.

He dropped it back into his pocket.

He walked out to where the horse waited.

★　★　★

The four killers came upon the small town in the growing heat of the morning.

It was a somnolent place, this town. It lay there as if the world had passed it by and its people were quite content that the world should do so. The stagecoach called there at infrequent intervals but people seldom got on or off. A wagon called more often bringing supplies.

But the countryside around was not too bad and folks cultivated it. The people were fairly self-sufficient. There were a few shops which sold the goods that the supply wagon brought. If a man had no money he could always barter his eggs, chickens, corn and other things for commodities like coffee and sugar and tinned goods.

This was a peaceful town.

It was never mentioned in the annals of the West so its name is not important.

What happened to it on that hot, somnolent morning when the four strangers came was something that the rest of the world did not know about, that old men could only tell about after the town had turned to dust.

19

Wolves in the Morning

Because they were wary they came in slowly, and they came in two by two.

Greg Burnette and Sam Konacky rode in first.

Cherokee Pete and Bat McGee waited on a rise overlooking the town and watched. They could see the winding main street. That was all the town was really, just the main street flanked by frame buildings and cabins and, here and there, even a tent. Here and there too, the dwellings had spread a little; extensions had been added to one or two stores, one or two saloons. Main Street had a lumpy look about it.

People looked at the two strangers, saw them for what they were. But hardcases had been through here before. There was nothing for them here, no bank, no rich ranchlands, no Wells Fargo strongroom, no regular stagecoach. They got eats and drinks for themselves and their animals and then they passed on to richer fields. Or maybe on to their ultimate destination, the outlaw hell-hole called Hangtown.

These two horsemen, the lean sandy-haired one and the little ratfaced one, were probably on their way to Hangtown now. They were dirty, travelstained, and their horses looked tired. They were probably on the run.

Ask them no questions, the townsfolk thought to themselves. Give them the usual impersonal courtesy, the usual impersonal service. They'll go the way all the rest went, the loud ones, the boastful ones, the scared ones, the sick ones, the quiet and deadly ones. They were passing through, they never had time to waste on a little town. They went on and the town was as it had been before they came . . .

★ ★ ★

Burnette and Konacky rode the whole length of the Main Street. Nobody took much notice of them, or pretended not to. The town went about its business.

The two men turned about and came back. They hitched their horses outside the saloon halfway down Main Street and they entered through the swinging batwings.

Little Sam Konacky was parched. All he had in his head was thoughts of a few drinks of hooch chased down by cool beer. His ratlike face was as relaxed-looking as it could ever be.

But Greg Burnette looked mean and felt mean. He was a gunfighter and a killer and he looked like a gunfighter and a killer. He was a wild one. He had shot up towns like this many a time just for the hell of it. He liked to see these smalltown marks stare at him, see the uncertainty or fear in their eyes. He didn't like to be ignored. He liked to make his presence felt.

He might not have been able to do that in this town . . . if it hadn't been for Ed O'Dowdy.

Ed O'Dowdy was an Irish bartender. He had learned his trade on 'Frisco's Barbary Coast among the jackrollers, the plug-uglies, the eye-gougers, the roustabouts who carried belaying pins in their belts and cracked skulls indiscriminately at the slightest provocation.

Ed had been one of the best all-round brawlers on 'Frisco's notorious waterfront. More than a few dives had been glad of his burly presence at their door or behind their bar.

But Ed had met and fallen in love with a saloon-keeper's daughter and they had married and, seeking a new life, had moved West. And Ed had settled in this quiet town and put his old roaring days behind him.

Ed ran a little farm outside town. His wife, Ellie and he had everything they wanted, except one thing. They had their love, their happiness, their farm, the goodwill of their neighbours and the other townsfolk, their peace of mind. But they didn't have the child they both craved; the son or daughter, it didn't matter which, who would delight their middle age and bolster their old.

Ellie tried to bear this child and died in the effort. For months afterwards Ed was like a man in another world, a gaunt creature who prowled the farmlands like a grey ghost. He wanted to die as Ellie had died. But it wasn't that easy. He was too tough; his spirit was too tenacious.

He let the farm go to rack and ruin and finally left it altogether and moved down into the town. He went back to his old profession.

He became a barman.

He became a barman in that very saloon which Greg Burnette and Sam Konacky visited one hot morning in the dusty town.

Out of all that quiet town the two killers had to pick that particular bar and a man who had never been pushed, who wouldn't be, who didn't care really whether he lived or died.

He served them and he noticed them. A couple of mean ones he thought. We haven't had a couple like that through here in a long time. Well, just let 'em start something, that was all.

Greg Burnette saw that the middle-aged, grey-faced barman had taken note of them. He had wanted to be noticed. But not in this way.

The barman was looking at him and Sam as if they were bugs he would enjoy crushing underfoot.

Greg Burnette was like a lobo wolf. He should have been left to prowl alone until he was shot down like a lobo wolf.

The old leader, Simmons of the ten-gallon hat, had had a strong personality and had been able to keep Burnette in check. He was a good planner and he helped Burnette to share in some rich hauls.

But now Simmons was dead and Burnette considered himself boss and he wanted a really good chance to prove this. It hurt his pride to be running from a posse, particularly when the fault had not initially been his own. There was nobody now to hold him in check. He had tasted blood back in Kansas City. His mean streak had been growing by the yard as they rode, as they were hunted.

He narrowed his eyes at the middle-aged bartender and said:

'What're you staring at, rube?'

The man did not answer, but did not drop his eyes either. He had a cloth in his hand and with this he began to slowly rub the bar down. But he kept his eyes on Burnette as if he intended to carry on a silent contest with him.

There was no fear in those eyes. They were old-looking beyond the years of their owner. They were tired. But they held no fear, only an abysmal contempt for this sandy-haired, hatchet-faced killer and all his kind.

Burnette's lips writhed back from his teeth. He drew his gun with the speed of a striking rattlesnake. He fired two shots. He put them one on each side of the bartender, close to his ears, smashing the long mirror behind the bar in dozens of pieces.

Ed O'Dowdy ducked down below the bar.

When he rose he had a gun in his hand.

Burnette hadn't expected this and he was taken by surprise, his own smoking gun hanging lax now at his side. O'Dowdy fired. He had never been a gunfighter and he was a poor shot. He missed Burnette, but Sam Konacky clapped a hand to the side of his face and blood spurted through his fingers as he screamed shrilly.

He went down.

Greg Burnette fired from the hip. He shot the bartender twice, once in the chest, once in the head.

Ed O'Dowdy crumpled up, fell out of sight behind the bar.

Burnette whirled, took a cursory glance at Sam Konacky. The little man was still, his face and head covered with blood.

Covering the few customers with his gun, Burnette backed across the saloon, through the batwings. He fired another shot through the saloon window before he vaulted on his horse and galloped him out of town.

The sound of the shots had carried up the hill to where Cherokee Pete and Bat McGee waited. They saw Greg Burnette riding alone along the Main Street in their direction. They broke from cover.

Burnette had left the end of Main Street when he saw them coming. He halted, waited for them.

His eyes were wild. He yelled: 'They got Sam. Let's take this town. Let's go through it, shoot it up.'

They drew level with him and he wheeled his horse, sent him back the way he had come, with the others now galloping at his heels.

They galloped through the town screaming and shooting. Very few people had yet realized what was happening. They were coming away from their houses and shops, moving towards the saloon to see what the shooting was about.

Many of them were caught in the open streets. A fat barber was shot down outside the front of his own establishment. He died quickly, his white smock marred with blood.

A little girl was shot in the arm. Her playmate, a red-headed boy, ran screaming in rage after Greg Burnette until Cherokee Pete's horse bowled him over, stunning him.

Windows were smashed. Doors and logs and clapboard fronts were riddled with bullets. The killers fired pointblank into a milling group of people outside the saloon.

There had been a rumour that the misery-ridden Ed O'Dowdy had committed suicide. This story was soon squashed. Another man died. More were wounded by shots and by flying glass.

Amid the holocaust Sam Konacky climbed unsteadily to his feet and clawed blood from his eyes. The bullet from the bartender's gun had only 'creased' him on the temple and knocked him unconscious.

The bar-room was empty and by the time it filled up again with panic-stricken people seeking cover, Konacky had found his way out through the back door.

But his horse was out front and his friends, thinking him dead, had ridden on out of town. Sam Konacky was left alone.

20

Guns of the Hunter

Darcy Kane heard the shooting as he approached the town. He halted his horse. After a bit of hesitation, a grin, a grimace, he pinned his deputy marshal's badge prominently upon his breast.

Come to think of it, he hadn't been properly sworn in, didn't know whether his badge really gave him any official standing at all.

He was soon to learn what the badge meant to other people, however.

Just outside Main Street two men stepped from cover of a privy and menaced him, one with a rifle, the other with a double-barrelled shotgun.

'What goes on?' demanded the tall rider, harshly.

The one man lowered his shotgun.

'Hell, are we glad to see you, Marshal!' he exclaimed.

Darcy said: 'I'm looking for four men . . . '

He didn't have to finish his sentence. The man with the rifle said:

'We've got one of 'em penned in the barbershop. He seems to have plenty of ammunition though an' he's a good shot.'

Darcy heard the rest of the misery-ridden story then, piece by piece, the two men recounting it to him as they accompanied him up Main Street.

The barbershop was in a stage of siege. Opposite to it men crouched in the windows and doorways of other establishments and, in the street itself behind carts and barrels and any other bulwarks they could find.

A man showed too much of himself and a gun spat viciously from a window of the barbershop. The foolhardy man's hat was skittered from his head.

'We better take cover, marshal,' said the man with the rifle.

Darcy got off his horse, led it into cover at the corner of a building. His two newfound friends and allies joined him, complete with rifle and shotgun.

'What's he like, the man you've got in there?'

'A little squeezed-up sorta fellah,' said the man with the shotgun.

Sam Konacky, thought Darcy. He said:

'Has anybody tried to get him from the back?'

'Kelly Trane, the blacksmith, tried. He didn't come back. That skunk must've got him. We're not gunfighters here, marshal. We're peaceful people.'

Darcy said: 'I'm going back a bit and then try to cross the road without being spotted. You two boys keep pumping lead into that barbershop . . . '

'Yes, marshal.'

'Count ten slowly while you're firing. And then stop and move among your people as best you can and tell them to hold their fire. Can you do that?'

'Sure, marshal.'

'I'm on my way then.' Darcy left them.

Back aways he crossed the road without a shot being fired in his direction. He moved quickly between two buildings, round a corner, along the backs.

Then, as he halted at the back door of the barbershop the barrage outside stopped abruptly.

Darcy drew his gun. With his free hand he tried the door. It was locked. Konacky must have locked it after he had taken care of the blacksmith.

There were a few more scattered shots from outside, as if Darcy's two friends had not yet given the word all round.

Darcy put a bullet in the lock of the door and kicked it open. He almost fell over the blacksmith whose bulk was sprawled just inside the door. The man moved feebly, was still alive.

His gun lay near him. Darcy bent and scooped it up. He darted over into the corner of the room.

The place was surrounded by mirrors, washbowls, swivel chairs. Darcy saw Konacky through one of the mirrors as the little man came through the curtain from the other room, a gun in each hand.

Konacky put two bullets into the still-moving back door before he saw the reflection in the mirror, the tall dark man whom he had thought he might never see again.

With a choked cry he whirled to face the man in the corner.

Darcy shot him twice.

Konacky went over backwards, one empty hand clawing the air, the other one still weighted by a gun. His thumb contracted on the hammer and the gun fired one last useless slug into the floor.

Sam Konacky lay staring sightlessly at the ceiling, his pinched-up face contorted in the last grimace of death.

So now there are three, thought Darcy Kane, looking down dispassion-ately at the body.

Konacky had been a little rat. He had died like a rat.

21

The Dead and the Living

Ed O'Dowdy, the Irish bartender-cum-farmer, had had many friends in the little town where he spent the happiest years of his life and a few miserable months too before he died.

In many ways he had been dead long before the bullet from Greg Burnette's gun let the soul free from the tough Irish body. He had died when Ellie died. Since then he had only been waiting for the real end, the end of the body he dragged with him from day to day through those last weary, fog-ridden months.

But for those last few moments before the bullets tore the living soul from him he had lived again. He had fought scum the way he had always fought scum in the old days. And he had died fighting, as any roistering fighting Irishman should.

The townsfolk mourned him. As they mourned the others who had died on that terrible morning in the sun and the dust. He had no kith or kin, they said; he had no close friends back at the Barbary Coast from whence he came. They would bury him here, they said, bury him with his wife on the little knoll overlooking the now disused farm that had once been their home.

Though the townsfolk did not know it, Ed O'Dowdy had had another friend in the West. Somebody who did not belong to the town. Somebody whom Ed did not speak about. For the name was notorious and, on his rare visits to the farm in the early days, its owner had much preferred to remain incognito.

He was Irish also and, like Ed, he came originally from the Barbary Coast. He was an uncle to Ed's wife, Ellie. His name was Shaun Bramar. He was wanted for killing a man in 'Frisco and two more in Kansas City who had tried to capture him for the bounty on his head.

Since then many more nefarious deeds, correctly or otherwise, had been laid at his door and the bounty on his head was the biggest laid on any man's in the West.

But who would dare to seek that bounty? For Shaun Bramar was known far and wide as the uncrowned king of that hell-hole, that 'wide-open' town, that outlaws' stronghold known sardonically as Hangtown.

Ed O'Dowdy and Shaun Bramar had been boyhood friends. It was through Shaun — older than his friend by about five years — that Ed had met Ellie and married her. Shaun had been best man at their wedding.

It was just after that that Shaun's wife ran away with another man and was abandoned by him, left to die of a lung infection brought about by ill-treatment and malnutrition. And Shaun had hunted the man responsible and shot him down like a dog.

And that was when the outlawry began, the bitterness, the savagery, the legend of the man with snow-white hair, a black heart and no soul, the mad Irishman who ruled the wild men and killers of Hangtown with ruthlessness and without pity, the man whom even the most dangerous of them feared more than they feared the Devil himself.

Perhaps only Ed and Ellie O'Dowdy saw flashes of the old carefree, good-natured Shaun. In the rare moments when, alone and like a thief in the night, he called at the farm to pay his respects to the only two people in the whole world with whom he could safely be his own self.

He had called there after Ellie's death. He had tried to reason with the half-dead lump of a man who greeted him.

Shaun had lost a wife too; he had lived; he had learned to forget. He was even a rich man now. He tried to get Ed to go back to Hangtown with him. But without success.

He reviled Ed to try and liven him up. He even struck trim. Ed told him dully to leave the farm and never come back. He hadn't seen Shaun again after that night.

Ed O'Dowdy had been dead almost a week before Shaun Bramar heard about it from a hardcase who had passed through the little town on his way to a hideout in the outlaw metropolis.

And by that time the man who killed Ed was already in Hangtown. And so were his two pards. And on his way there too, almost on the heels of the hardcase with the news about Ed, was the gambler turned hunter, the tall, dark man called Darcy Kane.

Here was another name that was becoming wreathed in legend. And, as is the way with all legend, the tales spread and grew and blossomed.

Shaun Bramar's informant had seen the man Kane too, had learned of his exploits.

It was said that this man had killed Simmons in a straight gunfight. And Simmons had been no slouch.

So Bramar set men to watch Ed O'Dowdy's killer, Burnette, and his two friends. And he set men to watch and wait for the arrival of Darcy Kane and he made a plan and a vow.

Darcy Kane had not known Ed O'Dowdy, had only seen the shell of O'Dowdy when he had out of courtesy attended his funeral and the funeral of the other murdered man. While all the while he was eager to start riding again, to get after the men who had done this thing and so many other things, to these people, to him.

Darcy had never met Shaun Bramar, only knew of him as a wanted killer and the King of Hangtown. By now Darcy had come to the conclusion that the four killers were making for Hangtown, that the three remaining ones would inevitably go on there. He might have thought momentarily that he might have to tangle with the King of

Hangtown before he could do what he had to do. But a dozen legendary Shaun Bramar's could not have turned him back from his objective now.

Darcy did not know that Ed O'Dowdy had been Shaun Bramar's boyhood friend, did not know that Ed's wife, Ellie, had been Bramar's niece.

Ed was dead and gone. Ellie too.

But there were the living.

Greg Burnette. Cherokee Pete. Bat McGee. Shaun Bramar. Darcy Kane. Five men. Drawn together by a strange destiny, a chain of circumstances. *Linked*.

But only one of them — King Shaun Bramar — knew the meaning of, the strength or the weakness of every link in that chain.

And Shaun, who liked playing checkers with men for living pieces, had a grim game to play.

But first he had to wait until all the pieces were together on the checkerboard that was Hangtown.

Three men thought they were now sitting pretty. Riches to be shared between only three of them instead of the original five. Another haul since the first one, and a diamond ring among this that they had since learned was quite valuable.

Among the misfits who had settled in Hangtown was an ex-jeweller wanted in Houston, Texas, for robbery and murder. For a trifling fee, he had valued the ring for Burnette and the rest.

And here they were then, the three of them, sitting pretty in the toughest town in the West, surrounded by people of their own kind who were quite capable of shooting up a posse on sight.

Sitting pretty. Not knowing what was in store for them . . . And another man who allowed them to sit pretty for a while and watched and waited and planned.

And a fifth man who was driven by fury and hate and an inner compulsion.

The hunter, the avenger, the instrument . . .

Five men moving toward a smoke-ridden Destiny.

* * *

But the malicious little Fates who waited on the sidelines decided to take a hand in things.

These Fates are the little devils who discover a man's weak spot and probe him there and goad him. As they played on Cherokee Pete's weakness for women now. As they led into his path a beautiful and immoral dance-hall girl who belonged to another man, a jealous man who was wanted for four murders and many other crimes. A big man, handsome as Cherokee Pete was handsome, and swarthy too, so that they might have been brothers.

The biggest dance-hall and bar in Hangtown was as notorious as the town itself. It was the kind of place, however, where an unscrupulous girl with the right kind of looks could get herself a stake quickly. They came from all over the States, the quick cats with the slow morals. And some of them were brought there. The dark beauty called Bridie was brought along by the tall dark killer called Saxon.

Cherokee Pete saw Bridie and she reminded him of Carmen, the filly who got away.

She leaned on the bar and she seemed to be alone. He went over to her and asked her to dance.

She was bored. Saxon was embroiled in a poker-game in the back room. She liked the look of this stranger. She went with him.

The night went on.

By the time Saxon put in an appearance Bridie was too drunk to care. And her companion was too mean to back down when Saxon tried to hand him his walking papers.

He drew his knife and flung it. But his aim was deflected a little by the woman leaning against him drunkenly.

The pointed razor-sharp blade, instead of penetrating Saxon's heart became imbedded deeply into his shoulder.

Saxon emptied his gun into Cherokee Pete's still-twitching body before he too collapsed.

He was still conscious enough though to spit bloodcurdling threats at Bridie as she bent tearfully over him.

She knew he would live to punish her and for this she was truly thankful.

22

The Men of the Town

Lin Carruthers was an emaciated beanpole of a man with only one eye.

He was Shaun Bramar's first lieutenant.

He it was who carried the news to the King about the demise of Cherokee Pete.

Bramar sat behind a huge mahogany desk in his office, the most luxurious office that anybody in Hangtown had ever seen. Not many, however, had been behind the office or in the rooms above it, and all this, they were told, was even more luxurious, fit for any king.

In very good taste too, said Lin Carruthers, a killer who came from a good Southern family and knew about such things.

There were a few girls too who had gained the King's favour over the years. They would have had a tale to tell. But invariably they were eventually sent away from Hangtown, set up in business elsewhere in some respectable undertaking like dressmaking or keeping a café or a select lodging-house.

It was known far and wide that the blackhearted Shaun had a certain code and part of this was that he always looked after his friends, old and new.

His current girl-friend was a dark, imperious Southern beauty called Amanda. She had come to town under the protection of a fancy gambler called Jupiter who, unfortunately, had gotten himself cut to death in a bar-room fracas not long afterwards. And quite openly and without any flurry Amanda had moved in with Shaun Bramar.

How long will she last? people asked. There were even bets laid on it, though very discreetly for Bramar was a proud man. Anybody who mocked him or insulted him, even behind his back and in the mildest way, was liable to be expelled from Hangtown for ever. And this was the least that could happen to him.

Seated behind that huge mahogany desk Shaun Bramar dispensed life and death, thunder and lightning, riches and poverty.

Sitting there in the finest broadcloth and silk and lace with his thick hair gleaming beneath the lamplight. With those large dark eyes like dead coals beneath the thick startlingly black eyebrows. With that clean-cut, swarthy face with the aquiline nose and the broad mobile mouth. With the broad shoulders, the deep chest, and the well-cut body.

Among the normal scum of Hangtown he was like a Viking among slaves and this was why he was king. People respected him. But they feared him, too, with a superstitious fear. He was the stuff of which legends are made.

* * *

'Well,' he barked as Lin Carruthers entered the office that night.

Deep lights flickered momentarily in the dead coals of the dark eyes, He had been working on accounts all evening and he was tired and frustrated.

What was money after all?

What could you do with money in a hell-hole like this? This hell of his own creating!

'Cherokee Pete just got himself shot into a couple of rag dolls,' said Carruthers.

'Hell, who's Cherokee Pete?'

'One of Greg Burnette's friends. One of the three you wanted watching.'

Bramar's interest quickened visibly. 'Kane isn't here?'

Carruthers shook his narrow, skull-like head.

'No, Saxon got him. He was fooling with Saxon's girl. He got Saxon with a knife. Saxon'll live.'

'Where were Cherokee Pete's two

friends at the time?'

'In a poker-game.'

'Watch 'em. I don't want any more shooting. Not yet.'

'They're being watched,' said Carruthers, unemotionally.

'So now there are only two,' said Bramar softly. 'Do you think Kane can handle them?'

'He handled Simmons,' said Carruthers.

'So he did. So he did.'

'He handled Sam Konacky. I knew Sam. He was a pretty fast little sidewinder.'

'It's time Kane got here,' said Bramar. 'I'm getting impatient. I don't want to handle this thing myself. It pleases me not to.'

'I know.'

'Have you passed the word around that there must be no interference when the time comes?'

'I have.'

'Do Burnette and McGee still know that Kane is on their trail?'

'Yes.'

Bramar chuckled, a toneless, humourless sound. 'Are they making anybody aware of their feelings on the matter?'

'They're bragging a mile a minute, if that's what you mean.'

'Pretty confident you mean?'

'Why wouldn't they be?' said Carruthers dryly. 'Even now they're two to one.'

'And they think they can get help if they want it too, I suppose.'

'Could be. There's a rumour that Darcy Kane got himself fixed up as a deputy marshal to make everything legal.'

'That was smart of him.'

'I'm not so sure about that. You know how people feel about the law in this town.'

'People in this town will do as I say,' said Bramar, softly and clearly. 'And you and the boys will see to it that they do.'

'We'll do that, Shaun,' said Carruthers. 'There's another rumour also that Kane has a posse with him.'

'It's the first I've heard of it.'

'Yeh. Anyway, I guess there must've been a posse in any case after the killings in Kansas City. But if I know anything about ordinary posses they'll have turned back by now. Only a wild man like Kane would have followed the boys this far, be prepared to follow them right into Hangtown.'

'Well, Kane's hardly likely to turn back now. I want a close watch kept on Burnette and McGee and on any friends they've got here.'

'We're doing that, Shaun.'

'You better send a couple of scouts out to check on Kane too. I don't want them to let him know he's being watched though.'

'I'll pick a couple of good boys, Shaun.'

'You do that, Lin,' said Bramar and bent once more over his books.

Carruthers knew he had been dismissed. He took his leave, closing the door softly and gently behind him.

Burnette and McGee had a couple of friends in Hangtown. A couple of professional killers called Rip and Masters. They would kill anybody for a price.

And, right now, Burnette and McGee had that price.

Burnette and McGee had begun to think that Darcy Kane was their own special jinx. He seemed to bear a charmed life too. As a gambler he seemed to be on a long winning streak. He was dicing with death and coming out on top every time.

Burnette and McGee were gamblers too. But not such good gamblers as Kane, a professional *par excellence*. He had always been an audacious bluffer.

Although he did not know it, even from a distance of miles he had Burnette and McGee bluffed completely. This was why they paid Rip and Masters to get him.

Burnette figured that he and his

bat-eyed pard could not leave town themselves. In fact, there seemed to be a sort of conspiracy against their leaving town. He had heard that already bets were being made on the outcome of the fight between Darcy Kane and him and his pard.

There was a rumour too, that Kane had reinforcements with him.

So Burnette sent Rip and Masters out to reconnoitre. And, if the odds weren't too great, they were to get rid of Kane and whoever was with him. Rip and Masters did not take foolish chances but if they decided to do the job completely, they would do it efficiently.

And Burnette and McGee wouldn't be connected with it at all. Here in town, taking part in an extended poker game; the eye of the whole town on them, so to speak, while they waited.

Rip and Masters always came and went like shadows. Nobody would notice they had gone; nobody would notice when they returned. They were like undertakers at a feast, slinking darkly and unobtrusively through the great hall among the myriad roistering guests, brushing them but lightly with the wings of Death.

23

Strange Incident on a Lonely Road

After the funeral of Ed O'Dowdy and the others, the people of the little town wanted to form a posse to accompany Darcy Kane to Hangtown.

But the tall gambler would not hear of this. He finally prevailed upon the townsfolk to play things his way for now. He said he would be back and, if he wasn't, it was up to them to do as they pleased.

He knew that if they came with him there would be a full-scale battle on the streets of Hangtown and most of them would die and he with them. And the men he sought might escape him after all.

But if he rode into Hangtown alone he stood a chance. He was willing to risk his own neck but not those of these good people who were not gunfighters but men of peace.

So he took the road alone. He left in the twilight and by full night he was well on the trail to Hangtown. He planned to camp just before he got there and then enter the outlaw town in early daylight.

His plans went well. He met nobody on the trail.

Then eventually he moved off the trail and found a small hollow and bedded-down there. He ate dry biscuits and drank sparingly from his canteen. He wasn't foolish enough to light a fire. He was dealing with three wolves who were quite capable of coming out here to stalk him, to bushwhack him out here in this dark loneliness, to bury his body, so that Darcy Kane would be literally wiped off the face of the earth.

He knew his horse would warn him if anybody approached. But by then it might be too late. So he did not light a fire.

He lay with his saddle for a pillow, his

gun beneath it, his hand on the butt of the gun. The night was eerie with pale stars and he lay in the shade of a small tree where he would not be so easily seen.

He must have slept.

Restless movements from his horse awakened him. It was still dark. The stars wheeled in the night sky. He sat up, his gun in his hand.

In the distance he heard the two shots. A short space of time between each one. Something deliberate-sounding about them. They sounded like revolver shots rather than rifle-fire.

Darcy rose to his feet. He put on his hat, one he had picked up in the little town he had just left. He saddled the horse and rode back the way he had come, back to where he figured the shots had sounded. He rode slowly and kept off the trail.

He thought he heard horses hooves in the distance and he halted his own cayuse gently. But then there was nothing but the soughing of the night-wind. After a bit he went on again.

His horse neighed suddenly and reared, almost unseating him. He slid from the saddle and crouched at the horse's belly, his gun out.

'All right, boy,' he whispered. 'All right.'

He could feel the beast trembling as if with an ague. Darcy stroked the smooth flanks. But the horse still trembled.

Nothing moved in front of them. There was a clump of undergrowth, a tall tree, and space all around.

To Darcy's right was a shallow dip in the ground and what looked like the bed of a dried-up pool.

Darcy threw himself sideways, away from the horse. He rolled. He came to rest at the bottom of the hollow and nothing happened. He felt rather foolish. The breeze soughed mockingly over his head, played with his hair. He had lost his hat.

He spotted it, picked it up, clapped it

on his head. Startled by his sudden movement, the black stallion was skittish again, snorting, wheeling away.

Darcy came out of the hollow. The horse spotted him again and stood waiting, trembling. He went over to it and stroked the smooth neck, murmured in the horse's ear. Finally, the beast became quiet but rolled its eyes whitely in the direction of the clump of underbrush, the tall trees.

Gun in hand, Darcy went over there.

In the centre of the underbrush two men lay side by side. They lay face downwards and they were both dead, shot neatly in the back of their heads.

Darcy rolled them over so that both their faces were upturned to the light of the stars.

He peered more closely at the white faces. Then, despite the contorted mouth, the terrible look of surprise and agony in the staring eyes, he recognized one of them.

He recognized the man because like Darcy he was a Southerner. *Had* been a

Southerner. A man of about Darcy's own age who was notorious as a cold-blooded killer, a professional, and who was known only by the appellation of Rip.

Darcy didn't know Rip's companion but guessed it was the partner he had heard of, the one who had been connected with Rip over the last few years and was known as Masters.

Both of the men still had their guns, nestling on their thighs in low-slung holsters. There was no sign of a struggle having taken place here in the under-growth.

Darcy straightened up, looked about him. No horses. But he moved now and came to the trail and there he found tracks. He figured that there had been four horses and they had been coming from the direction of Hangtown. One pair had caught the other pair up maybe.

All right then! Had the first pair been Rip and Masters?

The second pair catching them up

must have been well-known to the two killers. So well-known that they had been able to take them by surprise. They must have shot them here on the trail, then taken the bodies to where Darcy had found them.

Because he was still rather mystified, he did some more peering around and finally he discovered a couple of spidery trails in the dust where the bodies had been dragged. The murderers must have taken the two spare horses with them.

He went back to the bodies, to the horse who was standing quietly now.

Darcy mounted up. He left the bodies where they lay and rode on towards Hangtown.

Rip and Masters were no loss to anybody but he was still mystified by the manner and suddenness of their death.

Perhaps Hangtown held the answer.

★　★　★

216

It was morning when Lin Carruthers visited his boss once more.

Bramar was having breakfast. Carruthers stood respectfully before him, hat in hand. The dark Amanda sat on Bramar's right hand in a gorgeous red velvet robe and toyed with something small on a china plate.

She had given the one-eyed beanpole one disdainful glance and now acted as if he wasn't there. She was the king's woman and she had no truck with underlings.

Bramar chewed rhythmically, finally emptied his mouth. 'Well,' he said.

'It's important, Shaun,' said Carruthers tonelessly.

'Take a walk, Amanda.'

'But, Shaun . . . '

'Go on.' The white-haired man's voice was like a whiplash.

The girl cringed beneath it. She got up and left the room. She gave Lin Carruthers a nasty look as she left the room.

He ignored it. He was used to such

looks from Shaun's girls. He'd still be here when Amanda was gone and a few more fillies like her no doubt.

'I sent Gimbald and Lopez out scouting,' he said. 'They ran into those two sidewinders, Rip and Masters. They had located Kane, who's all on his lonesome. They were working on getting around behind him and dry-gulching him. Burnette and McGee were paying them to do this . . . '

'I might've known those two would try to pull some fancy trick. So what did Gimbald and Lopez do?'

Carruthers spread his hands, grinned mirthlessly with his narrow death's head. 'They took care of Rip and Masters.'

'Good. Did Kane spot them?'

'No. They got in front of him. They figure he'll be in town any time now.'

'All right, we'll let it play out the way it stands. But keep a closer watch on Burnette and McGee. They might begin to wonder what happened to their two tame executioners. They

218

might try an' leave town to investigate.'

'And if they do?'

'Just tell 'em I want to see 'em . . .'

Bramar paused. He tossed a cigar to Carruthers who caught it expertly. He had a lot of practice catching cigars over the breakfast table when he delivered his morning reports.

They lit up. Bramar puffed smoke in a blue cloud. Then he continued to talk, softly and reflectively now. 'Burnette and McGee killed Ed O'Dowdy, you know that, Lin. They've got to pay for that. I want to let Darcy Kane take first chance at them. He's certainly earned it. I've never met him but I'm beginning to feel a kind of fellow feeling for the man.

'If he doesn't get them I will. If he gets only one of them and is then dropped, I want the other one y'understand? He's all mine!'

'I understand, Shaun. The boys understand.'

'If Kane comes out on top I want him brought here. I want to shake him by the hand. If he's hurt I want him looked after like he was a prince.'

'That's all understood, Shaun,' said Carruthers. Bramar looked across the table at him. 'You're a good man, Lin. You've got breeding. I wonder what made you what you are.'

'It's a long story, Shaun.'

'And you've never told it, not even to me.' Shaun sighed. 'Well, I don't suppose you'll ever tell it now.'

He paused. Then went on again:

'We've all got our stories. All of us in this goddamned hell-hole.'

Carruthers' skull-like face did not change expression. But he thought, Shaun's getting old. He's older than I am and I feel hellishly old sometimes.

We're all getting old.

He knew how Shaun felt.

'All right, Lin,' said Bramar. 'Thanks.'

'No thanks are needed, Shaun,' said Carruthers mildly.

Bramar grinned with a flash of white teeth. The old devil-may-care grin that never reached the sombre eyes. Carruthers had never seen those eyes light up with humour.

He wondered what Shaun had been like before Hangtown.

What had he himself been like before Hangtown? *No!* — he didn't like to think about those days . . . Yes, he knew how Shaun felt.

'So all we have to do is watch and wait,' he said. 'And then watch again.' He gave a little spurt of toneless laughter. 'It should be good.'

He left the room, closing the door softly and gently behind him.

24

Ending and Epilogue

Though Greg Burnette and Bat McGee might have thought there was some kind of conspiracy against them afoot in this town, they never realized that even if they were to kill Darcy Kane their own Fate was irrevocably sealed.

They might have thought everybody in town was eager for them not to leave, for them to stay and meet Kane because there were so many bets being laid on the outcome. This was a gambling town. The outlaws here, the outcasts, the misfits would bet on anything. Whether a man lived or died, whether this man got the woman or that man; they'd bet on two flies climbing a window-pane, two bugs crossing a bar-room floor, two dogs fighting in the streets, two horses racing; bet on who could spit the furthest, who could shoot the straightest, the fastest . . .

This wager on a gunfight — two men against one — this was a wager to beat all.

The greatest joke about this wager, however, was shared only by the select circle that was closest to Shaun Bramar. They knew that if of the three protagonists Darcy Kane didn't win, nobody would win. Either way, Shaun would see that the men who were responsible for the death of his boyhood friend, Ed O'Dowdy, would die violently, the way Ed had died.

But Burnette and McGee must have sensed something. They had certainly one thing to worry about. And that morning in the room they shared together Bat McGee voiced his fear.

'I wonder what's happened to Rip and Masters, Greg. They should be back long before now.'

'Maybe they got cold feet,' said Burnette.

'That's not like them. They don't fall down on jobs. Besides, they said they needed the money.'

'Well, they can't have the money if they don't come back for it can they?' said Burnette nastily.

'Maybe Kane got them.'

'How could he? He wouldn't know they were after him. They had all the advantages. They're experts at that sort of thing.'

Bat McGee licked his dry lips. He wouldn't like Greg to label him yellow but he was a very worried man.

'There's something else, Greg . . . ' he hesitated.

'Oh, hell, what?'

'When I was out back last night I saw two of Bramar's men, Gimbald and Lopez. They looked as if they'd been out riding. They were riding in quietly round the backs. And they'd got two extra horses with them . . . '

'So?' Burnette was impatient.

'They looked like Rip's and Masters' horses.'

Burnette stared at him, his brow wrinkled. 'But that doesn't make sense.'

'I dunno, Greg. I've got a feeling that something's going on in this town that we don't know about. I don't stick at the tables like you do. I'm not such a good gambler as you. I lose a lot. I drop out when I can. I been moving around a bit on my own while you've been playing . . . '

'Don't tell me you think Cherokee Pete's killing was rigged or something . . . '

'No. That was just through Pete's cussedness. We got his money didn't we . . . ? No, but I've heard things since . . . You know that little town where we had that rumpus, where they say Kane got Sam? What's the name of it?'

'I don't know. Hell, it doesn't matter. A hole like that . . . '

'No, but I heard somebody say Shaun Bramar has friends in that town an' one of 'em got killed . . . '

'Oh, for Pete's sake, is it likely Bramar 'ud have friends in a dump like that? You hear all kinds of rumours and legends about Shaun Bramar. Anybody'd think he was some kind of god.'

'He's a pretty powerful man, Greg,' said McGee. 'I think we ought to get away from this town right away before Kane gets here. They say he might have a posse with him. There might be truth in that . . . '

'He won't stand a chance if he's got a bunch with him, you know that. We'd have the whole town on our side . . . '

'We haven't got it now, Greg. I feel it . . . '

McGee's voice trailed off.

Burnette had crossed to the window.

'Kane's here,' he said quietly. 'He's alone.'

★　★　★

Darcy had been surprised at the welcome accorded him when he entered Hangtown.

'Mr Kane's here,' said the man at the

livery-stable and a boy ran excitedly down the street.

'Let me see to your horse, Mr Kane,' said the hostler. 'My, my — he suttinly is a lovely beast. There's a bowl over there if you want to wash-up. An' my woman's getting a meal prepared if you want to eat.'

'That's swell of you,' said Darcy in surprise. 'I will wash. But I won't have anything to eat yet thank you.'

'Suit yourself, suh.'

Darcy had washed, was wiping himself vigorously when the boy returned and with him a very tall emaciated man with one eye. Darcy had heard descriptions of this man so there was no mistaking him. This was Shaun Bramar's lieutenant, Lin Carruthers.

He discovered he was right when Carruthers introduced himself.

'Shaun Bramar sends his compliments and says would you call and see him when you have time.'

The man's voice was sardonic, stung Kane a bit; so that he retorted, 'I have

227

some business to attend to first.'

'I know,' said Carruthers. 'They're here. You've only got two of 'em to worry about now. Cherokee Pete got himself killed.'

'Oh.' Darcy felt that his mouth was open. He closed it.

'Shall I tell Burnette and McGee you're ready for them, Mr Kane?' asked Carruthers gently.

'You can do that.'

The thin man turned at the door. 'Do you want any help, Mr Kane?'

'No, thank you.'

'I didn't think you would.'

Then Carruthers had gone as swiftly and quietly as he had arrived.

Suddenly Darcy remembered the two dead men back beside the trail. Had Carruthers been behind that, he wondered.

Had he been able to follow the thin, one-eyed man now he would have seen something else to puzzle him.

Carruthers knocking on an upstairs door in a hotel down the street and a

228

voice calling 'Come in.' Carruthers entering to be confronted by Burnette and McGee with drawn guns. Carruthers laughing, saying, 'You don't need those with me, boys. You will be needing them though. Met an old pardner of yours down the street. Fellah named Kane, Says he's ready for you. I said I'd deliver the message.'

Holding the door wide.

A little uncertainly Burnette and McGee holstering their guns passing through the door.

Carruthers closing it gently behind them.

⋆　⋆　⋆

Darcy Kane moved out into the sunshine of the dusty street.

It was quiet. There wasn't a soul in sight. The stage had been set for him. He felt he was being watched by dozens of unseen eyes.

He *knew* he was being watched. He saw the pale blobs of faces now

— behind windows, in the dusty apertures of half-open doors.

The sun was hot on the back of his neck. He felt as if he was being pushed into something. He feared some kind of trap; some kind of cruel and elaborate joke played by the devilish Shaun Bramar perhaps.

He was out in the centre of the street. A perfect target. *Being pushed*, he thought sardonically. Who am I kidding? Who's pushing me? Who asked me to come here? I've pushed myself all along. Because I had to, I'm here because I want to be and because it's too late to turn back now. If a dozen of them want to shoot me down where I stand let them get on with it. I'd like to see them first though . . .

He undid his coat so that he could better get at his gun in its shoulder-holster. He realized that he wasn't wearing his deputy marshal's badge. He took it out of his vest pocket, rubbed it quickly on his sleeve, pinned it to his breast.

There, that would give those buzzards something to shoot at!

But nothing happened and he walked on slowly.

Two men stepped off the sidewalk up ahead in front of him. They began to separate and spread out as they moved to the centre of the hard-baked, cart-rutted dusty street. He recognized the lean, sandy-haired Greg Burnette, the broader, squint-eyed Bat McGee.

This was what he had been riding towards then!

His eyes flickered from one to the other of them as he moved closer. This was what he had been approaching. He wanted the range to be just right.

They seemed to have reached the separation they needed and they remained still, facing him, their legs spread apart a little, their hands hanging.

They were seasoned gunfighters. This was their grandstand play. But they were not used to a man who kept moving, who kept coming at them.

They were not used to a man who kept walking with slow, measured tread, who walked erect with not the tiniest suggestion of a crouch, as they were beginning to half-crouch now, a man who wore his gun in a shoulder-holster instead of low-slung at his hip . . . They had seen that man draw from such a position. They knew how deadly fast he could be.

They had argued, as any gunfighter would, that the old draw was the best and the fastest, better than any fancy draw by any fancy gambler.

But they had to prove that now. And, though there were two of them, the odds on their side, the cards stacked in their favour, they each one had his private thoughts, each one waited. There was not time for any signal between them. They had to watch this man who kept coming towards them, who seemed as if he would walk for ever, walk *over* them if they did not stop him . . .

It was Bat McGee who broke first

and went for his gun.

Darcy Kane dropped on one knee and his right arm bent, the forearm like a striking snake. And when the arm straightened, the levelled gun roared and McGee screamed and spun. Then he fell flat on his back, his own gun still in its holster by the clawlike dying fingers.

Burnette had drawn too and he was very fast. But he was out-foxed by Kane's sudden lack of height. The tall, straight man was on one knee now, had suddenly become a dwarf. Burnette shot straight, but not low enough. His slug merely took Kane's hat off.

Kane might have used a shoulder-draw but he did not object to fanning the hammer of his gun in the time-honoured way. Still Burnette was harder to kill than McGee had been. Three shots hit him before he finally lay still. He had even managed to put another bullet perilously close to Kane's head before the dying fingers let the weapon fall.

Kane rose slowly to his feet. He holstered his gun. Automatically he brushed-off the knee of his trousers. The hand that had been so rock-steady a moment ago was beginning to tremble now.

★   ★   ★

The people were coming out upon the street, looking curiously at the two bodies and at Kane. It was as if they waited for a signal.

Kane bent and picked up his hat, beat it mechanically against his leg to shake the dust free. There was a neat hole at the tip of the crown. He put the hat back on his head.

He looked at nobody in particular, stood erect again, a fine figure of a man, still now, his dark handsome features set, melancholy, his arms hanging loosely at his sides.

Lin Carruthers came into view, with him a tall wellbuilt man with silver-white hair and strange dark eyes.

They came nearer and the tall man smiled but the smile did not reach those eyes, the saddest eyes Darcy had ever seen in a human face.

The silver-haired man held out his hand.

'Welcome to Hangtown, Marshal Kane,' he said.

Under the circumstances, it was rather a strange greeting. But it sufficed. Kane took the extended hand, returned the strong grip.

Now he could rest awhile before he returned . . .

To his beloved South. To St. Louis and his freedom and the return of his good name . . . to bargain for a black stallion he had grown to love . . . to a yellow-haired girl in a tumbledown farmhouse beside the Mississippi . . . to the big boats and the slap of waves and the sweet churn of a paddle-wheel . . .

We do hope that you have enjoyed reading this large print book.

Did you know that all of our titles are available for purchase?

We publish a wide range of high quality large print books including:
Romances, Mysteries, Classics
General Fiction
Non Fiction and Westerns

Special interest titles available in large print are:
The Little Oxford Dictionary
Music Book, Song Book
Hymn Book, Service Book

Also available from us courtesy of Oxford University Press:
Young Readers' Dictionary
(large print edition)
Young Readers' Thesaurus
(large print edition)

For further information or a free brochure, please contact us at:
Ulverscroft Large Print Books Ltd.,
The Green, Bradgate Road, Anstey,
Leicester, LE7 7FU, England.
Tel: (00 44) **0116 236 4325**
Fax: (00 44) **0116 234 0205**

The stage robbery had been accomplished by an old woman. Twine Fourch had never heard of a female being a highway robber before. He followed the trail all the way to a dilapidated log cabin up Stone Mountain. What happened after that no one could believe even after townsmen from Jefferson found the old log house and the skeletal dying old woman. But before the mystery could be solved there would be two unnecessary killings, a bizarre suicide and a lynching.

GUNS OF THE GAMBLER

M. Duggan

Destitute gambler Ben Crow arrives in Mallory keen to claim his inheritance, only to discover that rancher Edward Bacon has other ideas. Set up by Miss Dorothy, who had fooled him completely, Ben finds himself dangling on the end of a rope. Saved from death, Ben sets off in pursuit of Miss Dorothy, determined upon retribution. However, his quest for vengeance turns into a rescue mission when she is kidnapped by a crazy man-burning bandit.

SIDEWINDER

John Dyson

All Flynn wants is to be Marshal of Tucson, but he is framed by the territory's richest rancher, Frank Buchanan, and thrown into Yuma prison. Five years later Flynn comes out, intent on clearing his name and burning for vengeance. Fists thud, knives flash and bullets fly as he rides both sides of the law and participates in kidnapping and double-dealing. He is once again arrested for a murder of which he is innocent. Can he escape the noose a second time?

THE BLOODING OF JETHRO

Frank Fields

When Jethro Smith's family is murdered by outlaws, vengeance is the one thing on his mind. He meets the brother of one of the murderers, who attempts to exploit Jethro's grudge in the pursuit of his own vendetta. The local preacher, formerly a sheriff, teaches Jethro how to use a gun. With his new-found skills, Jethro and his somewhat unwelcome friend pit themselves against seemingly impossible odds. Whatever the outcome lead would surely fly.

SEVEN HELLS AND A SIXGUN

Jack Greer

Jim Cayman had been warned about Daphne Rankin, his boss's wife, and her little ways. When Daphne made a play for Jim and he resisted, the result was painful and about what he had feared. But suddenly matters went beyond the expected and he found himself left to die an awful death. Only then did he realise that there was far more than a woman scorned. He vowed that if he could escape from the hell-hole he would surely solve the mystery — and settle some scores.

CRISIS IN CASTELLO COUNTY

D. A. Horncastle

The first thing Texas Ranger Sergeant Brad Saunders finds when he responds to an urgent call for help from the local sheriff is the corpse of the public prosecutor floating in the Nueces River. Soon Brad finds himself caught in the midst of a power struggle between a gang of tough western outlaws and a bunch of Italian gangsters, whose thirst for bloody revenge knows no bounds. Brad was going to have all his work cut out to end the bloody warfare — and stay alive!